ASHES

www.chellebliss.com

CHELLE BLISS

USA TODAY BESTSELLING AUTHOR

Publisher © Chelle Bliss January 4th 2022
Edited by Lisa A. Hollett
Proofread by Read By Rose
Cover Design © Chelle Bliss
Cover Photo © Furious Fotog
Cover Model: Joe Adams

Print ISBN: 978-1-63743-031-6

www.chellebliss.com

CHELLE BLISS
USA TODAY BESTSELLING AUTHOR

MEN OF INKED: HEATWAVE SERIES
Same Family. New Generation.

Book 1 - Flame (Gigi)
Book 2 - Burn (Gigi)
Book 3 - Wildfire (Tamara)
Book 4 - Blaze (Lily)
Book 5 - Ignite (Tamara)
Book 6 - Spark (Nick)
Book 7 - Ember (Rocco)
Book 8 - Singe - (Carmello)
Book 9 - Ashes (Rosie)
Book 10 - Scorch (Luna)

CHELLE BLISS

NEWS, ROMANCE, AND CHAOS

Want a behind-the-scenes look at the chaos of my author life? Maybe you want early sneak peeks and other kickass treats.

CLICK HERE to join the fun or visit *menofinked.com/news*

…and as a special thank you, you'll receive a free copy of Resisting, a Men of Inked novella.

PROLOGUE

***

DYLAN

EVERY PERSON HAS A BREAKING POINT. Some people snap immediately, while others take years before they inevitably lose it.

I had put up with my father's shit for eighteen years, breaking a long time ago but resigning myself to my age and the limitations that placed on me and my ability to truly know freedom.

But for the last two years, I'd saved every penny I made, buying a bike and formulating a plan.

I am getting out.

I've had enough.

I'm done.

No longer will I continue to be his punching bag, taking the blame for all the wrongs in his life.

"Come with me," I say to my brother Ian as I jam everything I can into a backpack. "Don't stay here."

"I can't just leave," he says, sitting on the edge of my bed. "You shouldn't either."

"I can't do it anymore. I refuse to let this be my life."

His gaze drops to the black eye I'm sporting thanks to my father's drunken tirade last night. "Where will you go?"

"Don't care, as long as it's not here. Last chance to join me…"

Ian stands, following me to the front door and outside, but he doesn't grab his things. "I can't. This is home."

"This isn't a home, Ian. Life isn't supposed to be like this. He's not supposed to be like this."

"He said he'll get help," Ian tells me, sounding hopeful, even though there's no chance my father will get sober or change his ways.

I lift the backpack over my shoulder and stare at my brother as I stand next to my bike. "He always says that until he has another drink."

Ian kicks at the dirt near his feet. "Maybe this time will be different."

"It's never different. I want you to come with me. Don't stay here."

"I can't just leave everyone behind."

I shake my head, wishing I could talk sense into my brother. "No one cares about us. Callum, Finn, Sean, Nevin, and Quinn don't give a fuck what happens to you or me. Everyone's out for themselves. Don't be stupid."

"I'm not stupid, but I'm not a quitter. You may be willing to leave us behind, but I can't throw away my brothers as easily as you can."

"I'm no use to them if I'm dead," I tell him.

His face hardens as he lifts his chin, glaring at me. "If you leave, we might as well be to you. You hit that road, don't ever come back."

I take a deep breath, feeling the weight of his words. "Didn't plan on it, brother. Once I'm gone, I'm gone for good."

"You're an asshole," he bites out, looking at me with so much hatred. His mood has just shifted as quickly as our father's does after his first drink. Ian's just a kid, filled with so many hormones and emotions he doesn't understand.

I climb on my bike, ready to go, knowing I can't change how he feels and finally resigning myself to that fact. "I may be, but I'm going to be an alive asshole, living in peace without being someone's punching bag."

"Just go," Ian says, swiping his arm through the air. "I hope you find whatever you think is out there that's so much better."

"Ian, you deserve better too."

"Fuck off," he bites out and turns to face me before he makes it to the front door. "I hate you."

His words sting, but I've made my decision. No matter how much he hates me now, hopefully someday he'll understand why I have to go.

He'll have a breaking point too, and when he does, I hope he'll remember this moment and it'll finally hit him why I left and how it had nothing to do with him.

I walk my bike backward, ready to hit the road, when a loud giggle draws my attention.

The three girls next door are running around in the yard as their mother sits on a blanket, watching them closely. The oldest kid throws herself into her mother's arms, looking as if the world revolves around the woman.

An ache deep in my chest is hard to ignore as I watch the happy, perfect family for the last time. Their lives aren't filled with fists and hateful words. They walk in the clouds, not touched by the cold, harsh reality of everyday life.

One of the twins stops moving as soon as I start the engine. She looks my way, waving with a sweet smile on her face.

I curl my lip, jealous of her happy little life and perfect world she doesn't even know she has. She's a lucky little shit for it, too.

"Rosie, baby, come here," her mother calls, and for a moment, Rosie doesn't move.

She stares at me, her smile falling as I gun the

have as many life experiences as she can before it's too late.

At least, that is the bullshit line she feeds me, along with everyone else who bothers to ask.

The guy showed, so at least he didn't stand me up. But halfway through dinner, when I'd made it clear I wasn't looking to sleep with him tonight and was looking for an actual relationship, he excused himself to use the restroom and never returned. He left me with the check to pay, which included his entrée, the most expensive thing on the menu. Typical asshole.

"Darlin', I think it's ready to drink," the man next to me says, but it's barely audible because I'm so stuck in my thoughts.

I turn my head only slightly and give the man the side eye. He's not looking at me, beer to his lips, staring at the same line of bottles I was just a moment ago.

"Thanks, buddy," I say, but my voice isn't sweet. "Why don't you do you, and I'll do me. 'Kay?"

I go back to the bottles, ignoring the nagging feeling in my gut, the anger building in my veins toward all mankind that I want to unleash on something or someone, but am somehow holding inside.

A low, sultry laugh hits my ears. "It's more fun to do it with someone else, but if you wanna do you, I'll watch. Hell, you can watch me do me too if that's your thing. Whatever it takes to get that look off your face."

I swivel my entire body around, hand now gripping the thin stem of my drink, and glare at the man. With my chin raised, I announce to the side of his head, "It's not my thing. And while I'm at it, I'm sitting here, by myself, savoring my drink, trying to enjoy some peace and quiet, and you have to go open your big fat trap, invading my space and my brain with your bullshit. I don't know if your lines work on some women, but I'm telling you right now, I'm not some women, and it's not cute or called for. So, the little chat was nice, but again, buddy, you do you and I'll do me. That includes hands and mouths, and I prefer your mouth shut...tight." I don't move as I stand my ground, staring at his profile, shooting proverbial daggers with my eyes.

He turns his upper half toward me, finally showing me his face, and holy fucking shit, it's one hell of a face at that. Thick, bushy beard, impeccable skin which is somehow still rugged, full, luscious lips, and deep green eyes. I instantly hate him more than I did before I saw a face that has probably made more pairs of panties hit the floor than I could ever imagine.

I swallow as he raises an eyebrow, but his eyes stay soft and not threatening. "You done?" he asks.

"Are you?" I throw back, never breaking eye contact.

"Total dick move on my part. I should never talk to a woman like that. I'm sorry, but I had a shit day, and you're sitting here, looking sad and beautiful, and I couldn't help my stupid-ass mouth from inserting my boot right on inside. Forgive me for being the world's biggest asshole."

"First of all, having a shit day is no excuse for being a shit person. I think my shit day beats your shit day, and I was sitting here minding my business, enjoying my drink."

His smile goes lopsided and somehow cute. "You mean stirring it?"

I wrinkle my nose, lifting my chin a little higher. "I was thinking. It's something people typically do before they open their mouths."

The lines near his eyes deepen, and his smile widens and straightens. "You're salty along with sexy."

"Salty as fuck, man. Again, shit day, but that's my life."

His long, thick fingers wrap around his beer, and I dip my eyes, unable to stop myself. "Mine too, darlin'. Let me buy you another whatever the fuck that's called to make it up to you."

I shake my head. "If I have another, I'll be drunk."

"And maybe not so deep in thought."

"But I'll be drunk, and I don't drink and drive."

"Then I'll buy you a Coke or French fries."

I stare at him, thinking about his offer. I am still full from the meal I ate alone after the fucker ditched me, but… "Buy me dessert and I'll forget you were a creep."

He rubs the back of his neck with one hand, still holding the bottle with the other. "I'm not usually such a douchebag. I swear. It's just…" His gaze drops down, making a slow descent from my face to my toes. "You look like you're fishing."

"I'd never fish in these shoes." I peer down at my feet, loving the peep-toed stilettos I splurged on because every girl deserves something to make herself feel pretty. "You clearly know nothing about footwear."

He shakes his head, laughing as my eyes land on his face again. "I didn't mean fish fish, woman. I'm talking dick, and if you were casting a line, I was biting."

I narrow my eyes, grinding my teeth. "You'll never be lucky enough to bite my line, babe."

He doesn't seem fazed. "What's your name, beautiful?"

"What's yours?" I ask before answering.

"Handsome."

I roll my eyes. "What's your real name?"

"Dylan."

"Rosie."

He tilts his head, and his eyes study me, making me feel naked. "Wait a second…Rosie?"

"That's what I said, Dylan."

He leans back a little, arm resting on the bar, studying me for longer than what's completely comfortable. "Rosie Gallo?"

I nod and stop myself from releasing the sigh that's creeping up my throat. Great. He knows me. Of course he would in this small town. "The one and only."

"Fuck," he grunts as he straightens his back again. "Of all the hot bitches in the world."

I want to be mad because he called me a bitch, but the hot in front of that word nullifies the sting just enough for me to let it slide…for now. "And that means?" I cross my arms, unable to stop my lip from curling. "How do you know who I am?"

"Holy fuck. You grew up."

"That tends to happen with time. Who the hell are you, and how do you know me?" I repeat, seriously curious, because I have no memories or flashes of the wall of man in front of me.

"I'm Dylan Walsh, and you used to know me when you were a little girl, which you clearly aren't anymore. I also know your shoes are expensive as fuck and meant to get attention, and they got it…at least my attention. That's on top of your tits, ass, and killer hair. Everything about you screams high-class and probably a total pain-in-the-ass, high-maintenance chick. Also, I know your older sister, I remember your twin sister, I think your mother's a saint, and your father can be the biggest fucking asshole on the planet."

I blink, staring at him, but I recover quickly. "Dylan. Dylan. Dylan," I whisper, trying to jog some memory of him, twisting the martini stem in my fingers. "I'm drawing a blank although I clearly made an impression on you, but I have no memories of a Dylan. I do know the Walshes, and they're literally the biggest assholes on the planet, not my father. You got your shit backward and twisted, but I shouldn't be surprised if you are, in fact, a Walsh."

He lifts his leg, placing a single scuffed-up biker boot on the metal running along the bottom of the bar. "Your family always hated mine, and vice versa," he says before going back to nursing his beer.

"With good reason," I mutter, turning back to the position I was in before he started this weird conversation. "Your family isn't the most civilized."

"And your family are the most uppity people in the city. Always thought your shit didn't stink."

"What are you now...forty?" I ask that right as he's taking a sip of his beer, knowing damn well he's nowhere near forty, but wanting to give him a proverbial kick to the gut.

"Damn, woman. I'm thirty-five, and you're like twenty. Are you even old enough to be drinking that martini?"

"I'm twenty-four, thank you very much," I grumble before taking a long sip, polishing off most of my drink.

"Well, you look fucking amazing. Last time I saw you, I think you were eating dirt in the backyard with pigtails."

"One, I never wore pigtails. Two, I've never eaten dirt in my life. And three, you're still an asshole like the rest of the Walshes. What a pity."

"Why is it a pity?"

"Because you're not too hard on the eyes, but the one thing I don't do is Walshes. Therefore, you're on the no-fuck list for eternity."

"If I wasn't a Walsh—" he stops, setting his beer down "—you're saying you would've left with me?"

"Sure would've," I lie. "After the night I had, I could use a little reminder of why men are worth the hassle, and you may have been able to scratch the itch I have."

"I can still scratch it. No one has to know."

"I'll know, and that'll be enough. No Walshes ever. We swore an oath to my father to steer clear…"

"And a good girl like you always keeps the

promises she makes to her father?" he asks and waits for my reply.

"When it comes to the Walsh family…I sure as fuck do."

"Predictable," he mutters.

I lift the glass back to my lips, swallowing every last drop of the chocolate goodness. "I'm out. I've had enough males for one night. Thanks for the chat, Dylan Walsh."

"Thanks for the memories, darlin'," he says with a wink. "I'll be seeing you around."

"No, you won't. It's been over a decade, and I've never laid eyes on you until now. I don't see it happening again anytime soon."

"I lived out of state, but now I'm back. I'm sure we'll run into each other again soon."

"Don't hold your breath," I mutter, tossing a ten on the bar top before walking away, careful not to fall on my face in the impossibly high heels.

Do not fall. Do not fall.

I'd never live that shit down if Dylan fucking Walsh saw me go down in a blaze of glory. I lied when I told him I didn't remember him. I do, but I haven't thought about him since the day I saw him get in a fistfight with his father and take off on his motorcycle, the engine roaring until it faded in the distance.

Dylan Walsh is no doubt nothing but trouble like the entire Walsh clan. He is not the type of trouble I

dating another one," Luna adds, glancing up toward the ceiling.

"You say that after each breakup, but the uniform gets you every time," I remind her.

"No more military," Luna repeats with a straight face but lying through her teeth. "If I want a man in uniform, I'm going for a hot firefighter or cop. They don't get deployed or stationed clear across the country or world. I need someone who's going to be closer. I don't know how the hell I can be clingy with someone who's a thousand miles away."

"Yo. What the hell?" Carmello says, joining us. "In case any of you have forgotten, we're running a business. We have customers and appointments. I'd like to get out of here at a decent hour tonight."

Gigi turns to him and narrows her eyes. "Yes, sir, boss man. We know. We're between customers."

Carmello shakes his head. "Not Rosie. She has someone waiting for her in the consultation room who's probably ready to walk out by now. He's been waiting at least half an hour."

My back stiffens as I glance around at my family. "Why didn't anyone tell me?"

Gigi shrugs. "He wasn't on the schedule. He called asking for you before he just showed up. I told him you had limited time and could do a walk-in consult, but he'd have a long wait. He said he'd wait as long as necessary. And now, he's waiting as long as necessary."

"What do I have? Thirty before my first appointment?" I ask Lily, who's closest to the computer.

"You did, but they canceled," Lily says.

"Fuck," I hiss. "People suck."

"Ah. Such rainbows and sunshine this morning," Carmello teases with a smile.

"This is going to be an awesome day," Pike adds, hating when one of us is crabby and really hating it when a few of us are—like today.

"Maybe your consult will want the spot?" Lily says, trying to be positive like she always is.

"Probably not," I reply as I stalk toward the consultation room with my coffee in hand, shaking out my bad vibes. The last thing I want to do is pass on my attitude to my potential client and chase away business.

I rush into the room, saying, "Sorry you've waited so long," to the back of his head. "If I would've known I had someone waiting, I..." My voice dies as soon as he turns around and our eyes meet. I almost stagger back but somehow keep my feet planted.

"I told you we'd see each other again," he drawls with a smirk that's nothing short of salacious.

I grunt and move toward the other side of the table before setting down my coffee. "What are you doing here?" I ask, sliding into the chair across from him. "There're other ways to find me than wasting time at my business and costing me money."

"Who said I'm wasting your time or costing you money?" He relaxes into his chair, one arm bent and resting on the back, the other one extended across the table.

I stare at him, and he stares right back. "You're in my place of work."

"This is a tattoo shop, yeah?"

"You are correct, Einstein."

He lets out a little laugh, not bothered in the slightest by my dig. "I'm looking for some new ink, and I know—or at least heard—this is the best place in the area. I took a shot that you followed in your father's footsteps and were working here since there isn't much else to do in this shit-ass town. And, boom! Here I am, and you are too."

"Oh yay," I say sarcastically and fidget with my travel coffee mug because there's something about Dylan Walsh that has me a bit off-kilter. "You should've asked for one of the more senior artists like Pike or even Gigi."

"Nope," he retorts, shifting in his seat to lean over the table and close the small amount of space between us. "I wanted you, darlin'."

"Fuckin' fabulous," I grumble and push my coffee to the side because I need to meet Dylan head-on, and fidgeting of any kind won't be allowed. "Why don't you tell me what you want and where you want it. Let's start with the easy shit, and I'll see if it's something I can do before we move forward."

"You can," he says easily and quickly. "I have faith in you."

I raise an eyebrow. "Is it because of my tits or my ass?"

"Both," he replies without missing a beat. "But I also know you wouldn't be working here unless you were great. Inked doesn't hire shit, even if they're family."

"Fine. Tell me what you want," I say with a sigh, resigned to at least go through the motions with him. Whatever it takes to get Dylan Walsh gone sooner rather than later. I could bicker with him all day, but it wouldn't do anything except make him stick around longer than necessary.

"I want to get the first three lines of 'Do not go gentle into that good night,' along with some sort of decoration around it so it's not just plain script."

Somehow, I don't even blink. I never would've pegged the man in front of me for a poem type of guy, but here he is, asking for one of my favorites tattooed on his flesh forever. "Can you elaborate on the decoration? And do you want fancy script or something more like a typewriter font?"

He thinks for a minute, his eyes never leaving

mine. "I like the idea of a clean typewriter font. As for decoration, I'll let you pick."

"So, pink flowers, then?" I tease, hoping it's enough to chase his ass away.

"Whatever you think works best. I trust you."

"Why?"

"Why what?" he asks.

"Why do you trust me?"

"Because you're the artist."

"But you're...you're you and covered in tattoos, and nowhere on your skin are there any other flowers, especially pink ones, but you'd let me do it?"

He nods. "Why the fuck not?"

"Because I said pink."

He tilts his head to the side and looks at me funny. "And?"

"You're not a pink guy."

"Darlin'," he whispers, adjusting himself in his seat as he gazes across the table at me. "You don't even know what kind of guy I am, but if you think pink is good, I'm all for it."

"You're nuts," I mutter.

"Never claimed to be playing with a full deck, especially where you're involved."

I roll my eyes. "There're a lot easier ways to get laid than having pink flowers permanently inked on your flesh."

"Name one," he tells me.

I shrug. "Go to a bar and pick someone up. I'm sure there are plenty of women who would take you up on the offer."

"Tried that last night. Didn't work." He smiles, and damn it all to hell, I can't help but laugh.

"You're an idiot."

His smile only grows wider. "We doing this or what?"

I can't bite back the sigh. I have no excuse. I have the time since my first client canceled, and although Dylan can be a dick, his money is as good as anyone's. "Yeah. Give me thirty minutes to draw something up, and we'll do it if you have time now."

"Got nothing but time, sweetheart."

"Great."

"Great," he repeats.

"You want to stay in here or…"

"How about I go get you and me a fresh cup of coffee, and I'll come back in thirty to get this going?"

"You don't need to do that."

"I know I don't need to do that, but I could use a cup and I'm not a selfish prick who isn't going to bring you back a cup too. Unless you'd rather have something else."

"No. No. Coffee's fine, but just so you know, you're still not getting in my pants," I tell him as I rise from my seat.

"I'd be disappointed if all it took was a cup of

coffee, darlin'," he says as he stands and moves toward the door before I can, blocking my exit.

I'm inches from him, my neck craned back, staring up at his handsome, rugged face, itching to see if the hair on his jawline is as coarse as it looks. "You wanna move?"

He shakes his head and doesn't budge. He doesn't reach out to touch me. He doesn't do anything but stare down at me, making my heart flutter and my belly flip. "You feel it, don't you?" he asks softly.

"Feel what?" I lie, somehow stopping my voice from cracking.

"The electricity. The connection. The whatever there is between us in this room now and last night."

I wrinkle my nose, but I don't look away. Show no fear. Give no information. "I have no clue what you're talking about, Dylan."

"Rosie," he whispers softly, making the flip in my belly turn into an Olympic sport. I don't flinch as he reaches up, touching my jaw with the pad of his thumb so lightly goose bumps break out across my flesh. "You feel it."

"I…" I start to say, but the words die as his hand falls back to his side and he slides out the door, leaving me standing in the consultation room alone.

"Fuck," I hiss, bending over at the waist and placing my hands on my knees as if I've been sucker-punched in the gut. "This can't be happening to me."

I want Dylan Walsh. He knows it, and now I can't deny it. There is an electricity between us, a connection I'm going to have a pretty hard time denying as long as he's around.

I have only one way to stop anything from happening between us.

Distance.

"Rosie?" Gigi asks, her voice rising on the last syllable. "You okay? Did that guy do something wrong? Because I'll totally go after him and beat his ass."

I don't rise, staying hunched over to avoid her gaze. "No. He didn't do anything wrong, sis. He was fine. I just think I… I don't know. Maybe I ate something bad or I'm getting sick. I don't feel well suddenly."

Her hand is on my back a second later, rubbing small circles like Mom did when we were little and didn't feel well. "Why don't you go home and rest? We'll cover your customers or reschedule them."

"But he'll be back in thirty."

"Big design?" she asks, still comforting me and my lying mouth.

"No. It'll take two hours max depending on how intricate he wants to go."

"What's he want?" she asks.

I tell her the basics, but I do so standing up

instead of staying crouched over like a weirdo. "You sure Pike has time?"

"For something that small, he can totally make it work before his next appointment. If not, one of us will handle it. I'd rather you go home and rest than overdo it and make yourself sicker."

"You're the best," I tell her, feeling like a selfish asshole, but it is the only way I can think of to put that important distance between Dylan and me.

"Now, go. Get some rest and text me later."

"I will," I tell her, giving her a quick hug. "Thank you for this."

"That's what family is for, babe. We always have one another's backs."

If she only knew the real reason I was ditching, running away from the man who was bringing me coffee and was about to let me put pink flowers on his skin. "I got yours next time."

"Wouldn't expect anything less." She smiles.

I don't waste any more time, grabbing my purse and phone, leaving my coffee behind. I'm out the door and in my car, running away like a coward.

3

ROSIE

"So, is there something you want to tell me?" Gigi asks over the phone, and her voice is filled with attitude. It's the same tone I hear from my mother when she knows something but wants me to be the one to say it.

"I don't know what you're talking about." I will die on this hill of deceit.

"The man who was here…"

"Was Pike able to squeeze him in?" I ask, still ignoring her fishing attempt.

"No," she sighs. "He said he only wants you to do it."

"Damn," I whisper. "Did you put him on my schedule?"

Please say no. Please…

"Yeah. You had an opening tomorrow."

"Fuck," I mutter, covering the phone with my hands so she doesn't hear.

"Explain," she says to me, because naturally, she heard what I said since, like my mother, the girl hears everything.

"About?" I ask, playing dumb.

"Rosie."

"Gigi."

"Dylan Walsh."

"Oh, is that who that was? I had no idea."

There's silence. Not just normal silence, but the type where she's waiting for me to give up on lying.

"He's a paying customer, whether we like his family or not," I tell her, surrendering.

"You knew who he was, and this wasn't the first time you've seen him recently. He's also the reason you faked that you were about to shit your pants or throw up and ran out of here like your ass was literally on fire."

"That's not true."

"Dylan was never my friend, but we had a brief chat when he came back and you weren't here. I'm telling you right now... Do *not* get involved with that man."

"I'm not. Jesus." I collapse back onto my bed and stare up at the ceiling, throwing my arm over my face.

"Um, he came here looking for you. Only you.

What aren't you telling me?" she inquires, not giving up.

"Nothing. I ran into him at a bar. He talked to me for a total of five minutes, and that was it. He showed up today and threw me for a loop. I made it quite clear that I wanted nothing to do with him, Giovanna."

"He wants something to do with you, and Dad will have a massive coronary. He hates that family, and Dad likes everyone."

"I had a really bad date, and Dylan was at the bar while I nursed a martini. We talked. I left. That was it."

"He's cute, though, isn't he?"

"He's okay," I reply.

"Okay? He was okay in high school. Now he's all badass biker, throwing off those sexy alpha vibes that would draw in almost every chick within a ten-mile radius. He's more than okay, Rosie. He's downright dangerously handsome."

"He's also a Walsh and a no-go. I don't care how fucking hot he is or how much he makes my belly flip, it's never going to happen."

She gasps. "He makes your belly flip?"

"It means nothing," I mutter into the crook of my arm.

"Pike, Dylan makes Rosie's belly flip," she tells her

Dylan is and has always been so much older than us."

"Age is just a number."

I wrinkle my nose. "Second, his entire family is a shitshow."

"Chaos can be fun."

I roll my eyes at her but keep on talking. "Third, he's always been bad news. I don't have many memories of him, but the ones I do have don't give me the warm fuzzies."

"Everyone has a past, Ro. People change over time."

"And last, he's just a client looking for some ink. Nothing more."

She stares at me, studying my face in that silent way she often does. "We'll see about that," she says softly. "Have you looked him up online?"

"No." I narrow my eyes in warning. "And neither will you."

"Sure," she mutters, lying to me as she lifts up her phone.

"Lulu, I swear to God…"

"I'm just reading the text messages I missed. Calm the fuck down, Ro."

I tip my head back onto the cushion and stare up at the ceiling fan. "Whatever. Just don't start no shit where there is no shit."

"Would I do that?"

"Yes," I breathe. "You so would."

She snickers. "But what would it hurt to do a little online stalking?"

"Luna."

"What? Knowing a man like Dylan Walsh, he probably has zero social media presence anyway."

"I'm sure he's been too busy being in and out of prison his entire life to bother taking selfies and posting profound thoughts."

She shifts in the chair, getting more comfortable. There's silence for a few minutes, and I close my eyes, taking in the brief moment, knowing she's about to get chatty again. Luna never stays quiet for long.

"Well, you want the good news or the bad?" she asks.

I snap my head upright and glare at her. "What did you do?"

She gives me her big doe eyes over the top of her phone. "Nothing," she mutters.

I narrow my eyes. "Luna."

"What?"

"The bad."

She smiles. "It's not that bad."

"Quantify *that bad*."

"So, I may have found Dylan's social media."

My eyes widen and my back stiffens. "It's been under a minute, and you're already stalking him?"

"It literally takes a few seconds, Ro."

"What did you do?"

Her smile becomes more devilish. "The lanky stoner kid turned into one hot piece of ass." She whistles. "Like, shockingly high levels of hot. I'd so f—"

"Stop." I hold up my hand. "Don't say it."

"He's delish, Ro."

"Don't change the subject. What did you do?"

"I *may* have liked a few of his posts."

I gasp, horrified. "Jesus fucking Christ, Lu. Now he's going to know."

"Know what?" she asks innocently, but she knows exactly what she did and why she did it. She wanted to force this because one thing Luna loves more than talking is drama, especially when it's not in her life.

I jump up from the couch and start to pace. "Why the hell would you do that?"

"He won't even see it. He's probably like every other man in the world and doesn't even look at his social media. Relax, Ro. Breathe."

I stop moving, cross my arms over my chest, and glare at her. "And what if he's not like the others?"

She shrugs. "Then he'll know *I* liked his posts."

"After fifteen-plus years, you just randomly like his posts?" I grunt. "He'll know it's because of me, and then he'll think I like him, when I've done everything possible for him to understand there will *never*—and I mean *never*—be anything between us."

"It's a like, not an invitation to sex. Jesus, you're so

dramatic. You're going to give yourself a stroke before you're thirty."

I give Luna the middle finger before walking to my bedroom, closing the door, and shutting Luna and the world out.

"Bitch, you haven't been laid in so long you're going to grow cobwebs between your legs. You're too hot to sit alone, watching television every night, without a man at your side. You need to put yourself out there. I don't care if you've had your heart broken. It's time to start thinking like a man."

I throw my pillow at the door, and it bounces off, skidding across the floor before coming to a stop near the end of my bed.

"Men don't give a shit about our feelings. They just want pleasure. Dylan looks like a man who enjoys his pleasure and probably dishes it out with very little effort," she says from the other side of the door.

"Go away, Luna," I grumble before cursing under my breath.

"You'll thank me someday, bitch. Without me, you'd have a very dull and sexless life," she tells me before I hear the light patter of her footsteps as she finally leaves me alone.

"Asshole," I whisper.

Luna's always been the wilder one. Without her, I'd have a very calm life, not one filled with constant drama and the endless parade of men who come through our apartment like she's interviewing them for a job.

If I didn't love her...

I sigh, throwing my arm back over my face and letting my bed envelop me. A small sliver of me has been lonely, but that doesn't mean I want Dylan Walsh in my life. I steer clear of trouble, leaving that nonsense up to Luna, while I play life safer.

My time on this earth may have been boring in her eyes, but I enjoy the hell out of every tedious moment. I live without regrets, unlike my twin. She's left a path of destruction and a wake of broken hearts and gossip trailing behind her.

"Oh my God," she screeches from the living room.

She's trying to make me come out, but there's nothing she can say to do that.

There's a knock on my door followed by the jiggle of the handle. "Rosie, stop being a shit in the pants."

"Fuck off."

"Guess what?" she asks.

"Don't care," I say back.

"He messaged me," she says in a singsong voice, and my stomach rolls, barely catching up as I fly off the bed and head toward the door.

"I'm going to kill you," I tell her as I undo the lock and fling open the door.

She's smiling, leaning against the wall across from

my room. "Someday, you'll thank me," she says, waggling her eyebrows and holding out her phone for me to see.

Dylan: Hey, Luna. Shocking to see you on here. Tell Rosie I said hey and for her to shoot me a text.

"Fuck me," I whisper, shaking my head.

"If you're lucky…he will," she says with a laugh.

"I hate you."

"You love me."

"No, I don't."

"Yeah, you do. I'm going to give him your number."

My eyes widen. "Don't you dare."

She types away on her phone as I try to snatch it from her fingers, but the little bitch moves faster than me. "Done," she announces, tossing the phone on the couch across the room as soon as she makes her way out of the hallway. "Can't take it back now."

"You have no idea what you just did," I groan, my shoulders sagging forward and my stomach still rolling.

She crosses her arms, giving me the smuggest smile I've ever seen on her face. "I do, and someday you'll thank me for it, too."

4

DYLAN

My brother Finn is silent as he nurses a beer, and he's barely looked at me since he sat down.

I pick at the label on my bottle, letting him work through whatever fucked-up notions he has of the past.

He's made it clear he felt abandoned by me, but the damn kid was only twelve when I left. I couldn't very well throw him on the back of my bike and take off without a destination in mind. I could barely feed myself, let alone another mouth.

"Seventeen fuckin' years," he whispers. "Just gone. Poof. Vanished like you died and never looked back."

I turn in my stool, staring at my younger brother's profile. He has a scar on his temple near his hairline where my father no doubt threw something at his head for no damn good reason. My father got off on hurting anyone near him, even his own kids.

"Why didn't you leave, Finn?"

He swings his eyes to mine, and they're filled with anger and a world of hurt. "Why didn't you fucking take me?"

"I couldn't," I tell him, although he knows this. We've had multiple conversations over the almost two decades, but this is the first time we've been in the same room.

"Bullshit," he snaps. "You could've thrown me on the back of your bike. Dad never gave two fucks about us. It's not like he would've sent the cops after you for kidnapping me."

"You were a little kid, Finn. What the hell was I going to do with a twelve-year-old on the road? You had school and your friends. I couldn't uproot you from your life for God-knows-what I'd be doing and where I'd be going. I had a hard enough time surviving myself, let alone with a little kid in tow," I explain, but I know I'm getting nowhere.

His eyes grow harder, and the anger only deepens in him. "You look like you survived pretty damn well."

"It hasn't been an easy seventeen years."

He grunts, glaring at me as he takes another sip of the cheap-ass beer he ordered.

"I did shit I never thought I'd do. I thought life would get easier when I left this town behind me, but that was a big fucking lie. I had a hard enough time keeping myself alive, and I never would have made it with you on the back of my bike. We both would've died on the streets instead of sitting here, drinking a beer now."

"Seventeen years later," he says through gritted teeth, stuck on the amount of time I've been gone.

"I'm sorry," I tell him. Words I've never spoken in all the time I've been gone. Words that have power over many people and hopefully my brother too.

"Do you have any idea what life was like when you left?"

"Shit, I suppose."

"He turned all the anger he had for you on to us. Me, Callum, Sean, Nevin, Quinn, and Ian. We all had our spot as the main target for his anger. Nevin was the only one who did something about that shit, making sure it never happened again. Ruined his life over that asshole. Still paying the price for protecting us."

"I saw him last month," I say.

"How'd he look?"

"Like shit," I mutter.

"Heard prison could do that to a man."

"He'll be out in a few months."

"Ten years gone because he couldn't take the beatings anymore and decided to put good ole Dad in the ground instead of taking his fists. He never should've been put away for protecting himself or anyone else."

My stomach tightens as a tidal wave of guilt crashes over me. "I know, Finn."

"But everyone in this shit-ass town thought we were all low-life dirtbags. They had no idea what happened in that house and only saw Dad as a poor single father to seven young boys, all abandoned by their mother at an early age. It didn't matter to anyone that he beat us on the daily. Nevin was the only one who had a set of balls on him to make things stop. It should've been you. You should've been the one to save us. You should be the one sitting in jail right now, not Nevin."

"I should've stayed to protect you guys."

"Ain't no lie, but only a coward cuts and runs, and you, Dylan, are a coward."

His words are like a punch to the gut. I was a fucked-up eighteen-year-old when I left, high on coke, weed, and whatever else I could get my hands on at the time. I'd been a victim of my father's attacks for over a decade, and all I wanted was out. I needed freedom, and somewhere in the back of my stupid-ass mind, I thought if I left, my father might somehow change...that his anger would simmer, and he wouldn't throw hands as easily as he had.

"You didn't even call to see if we were okay."

"What the fuck was I supposed to call? We didn't

have a phone at the house, and no one had cell phones. Was I supposed to send up a Bat-Signal or some shit, Finn?"

"A letter would've been nice. Something. Anything. Just gone. Forgotten. Like we were dead to you. But it's okay. You were dead to us too."

Time hasn't healed old wounds. It never does. I already know, no matter what I say to Finn, he's never going to forgive me. I'm wasting my breath even trying to explain myself. He was lost to me the day I left.

"Why even bother coming back?" he asks.

"Quinn called me last month and told me what was going on with Ian."

"We have it under control. We're taking care of him. We didn't need you blowing back into town and offering your help out of nowhere. You haven't given a shit for seventeen fucking years, Dylan, and we sure as fuck don't need it now."

"Ian wanted me here," I bite out.

"Clearly the cancer has fucked with his head."

I push my beer forward, no longer in the mood to drink or listen to my brother's verbal assault. Standing, I reach into my pocket and peel off a ten before tossing it on the bar. "Doesn't matter what you think or feel, brother."

Finn sneers at me, but I'm not putting up with his shit. I've spent the second half of my life not putting up with anyone's shit, and I'm not about to start now. Blood or no blood, I'm not going to listen to his shit.

I lean over, getting right in his face, making sure he hears every word I'm about to speak. "I was asked to come, and I came. Simple as that. You don't need to like it. You don't need to see or speak to me. But if Ian wants me here, and Quinn too, then I'm fucking staying. You have a problem with that...it's your fucking problem. You steer clear of me, and I'll sure as fuck steer clear of you. Got me?"

He barks out a bitter laugh, his eyes sparkling and filled with hate. When he rises from his stool, we're eye to eye, the same color green staring back at me. "I ain't steering clear of shit. As long as you're sharing the same air as me, I'm going to make you as miserable as I possibly can. You don't get to abandon us and then ride back in like some bullshit hero."

"Whatever, Finn."

"Piece of shit," he mutters. "Worthless piece of shit."

"Glad to see you sound just like Dad, even picking up on his phrases and making them your own."

His eyes flash, and he pushes a single hand against my chest, trying to knock me backward. "Want to settle this outside?" he's quick to ask.

I keep my feet planted against the sticky tile floor, not moving from his piss-poor excuse for a shove. "Ah. You even settle your feelings the same way too. You need to work on that shit, brother. It's not a good look on any man, especially a Walsh."

"You're not worth the night in jail," he replies, dropping back into the stool before his hand finds his beer. "Get the fuck out of my sight, brother," he says, the last word sounding more like profanity than a term of endearment.

"You need me, you call. Until then, I'll stay out of your way, and you stay the fuck out of mine," I tell him, drawing the line of where our relationship stands and will remain for what will probably be an eternity.

I don't think there's anything I can do for Finn to forgive me for leaving. He's had too many years to hate me, twisting the memories from that time into whatever bullshit he needed to survive. Whatever connection we had died the day I left. That is on me and something I have to live with every damn day.

He doesn't so much as look at me. It's as if I no longer exist to him. But as soon as I start to move away, he says, "You've been here a week and somehow feel you've earned back your spot in this family. You haven't. Doesn't matter what Quinn or Ian says, they feel the same way too. You're an outsider. Not family. Not our brother. You ain't shit anymore."

There's nothing more for me to say. He's said his piece, telling me how he's felt for the last seventeen years without me around. "You know where to find me if you need me."

He lets out a bitter laugh. "That's ripe."

I stalk out of the bar, eyes on me from many of the people in my past, looking as if they've seen a ghost. As soon as I step outside, I turn my face toward the starlit sky and inhale the salty, humid air, cursing myself for coming back to this shithole after I said I'd never step foot in this state again.

If it weren't for Ian's cancer and need of a bone marrow match, I wouldn't fucking be here either. None of our other brothers was a match to him, and while I was the last person to be asked, I came as soon as he called. I may have left them all behind in the past, choosing self-preservation over abuse, but I'm not going to turn my back on him again. This is a matter of life and death, and I won't let my brother die because I don't want to hear the wrath from the others.

"Looked rough in there, sugar," a voice says from behind me.

I spin around, seeing a woman who was once a pretty girl, but is now a shell of her former self. A woman I once thought I loved, sliding between her legs on the regular when we were in high school. "Shanda?"

"Yeah, baby," she says, throwing her cigarette on the ground and smashing the burning end with her beat-up high heel. "Never thought I'd lay eyes on you again."

I don't move toward her, something I would've done in the past. "You're as surprised as me."

She has no problem walking toward me, her eyes sliding down and up my body, studying every inch. "You're looking good, though, Dylan. Better than you did when I last saw you."

As she gets closer, I step back, not wanting any part of the train wreck she looks like she is. "You look…" I don't even have it in me to lie. Her face is pockmarked, no doubt from the countless years of drug use.

"You feel like going at it once more for old time's sake?" she asks without shame.

I shake my head, flipping through all the ways I can turn her down without her causing a scene. "Can't, babe. Although the offer is tempting, I have a girl."

Shanda had been sweet, but she was always about the drama, and I'm not in the mood for more bullshit than I have already experienced tonight.

"I won't tell anyone," she replies, still having zero shame, smiling at me with her checkerboard grin.

"I have to go," I tell her, taking a few steps backward.

"Maybe another time," she calls out as I move away from her.

"Yeah, maybe," I lie, turning around and making my way toward my bike, leaving the past where it belongs—in the darkness.

When I finally kick off my boots at the door, I collapse into a chair on the front porch, a jumble of emotions running through me. I never thought I'd be back here again. The place where so much bad shit had happened, and any happy memories were few and far between.

I'd taken more than a few beatings in this very spot, my body bent over the railing as my father lashed me with his belt until his arm grew too tired to swing the leather again.

"Hey," Ian says as he pokes his head out of the rusted screen door. "Y'alright? Need a beer or anything?"

"Nah, kid. I'm fine. Do you need anything?" I ask in return, because he's the sick one and clearly the nicest of all the Walsh men.

He steps out onto the porch, the screen door slamming behind him as he leans on the railing and turns to face me. "You're here. That's all I needed."

I have no doubt if one of my other brothers had been a match, I wouldn't have been needed or wanted. I probably never would've heard about Ian's battle with cancer either. All my brothers feel like Finn does, but they aren't as easy with sharing their feelings, even when they're filled with hatred.

"You feeling okay?" I ask him, noticing the slight wince on his face when his one hip touches the railing.

"Fine. My body's just shit after the chemo and radiation. It's like catching a beating, but instead of the pain being in one area, it's everywhere and deep in your bones. Never felt a pain like it. Never want anyone else to feel it either."

The remnants of the little boy I left behind are still there. Glimpses of his childish features still dot his face, but they're older and weathered.

"I wish I could do more," I tell him, hating the look of pain and sadness in his eyes.

He raises one arm, brushing his strawberry-blond hair away from his eyes. "You're doing what I need, Dylan. Once the procedure is done, hopefully my body will start healing so I can get back to livin' instead of dyin'."

"No doubt," I whisper, unsure of what else to say.

He grimaces as he shifts his weight from one leg to the other. "I need to go lie down. You going to be okay out here alone?"

"I'll be fine, Ian. Go rest," I reassure him. "Holler if you need anything."

He gives me a sorrowful smile before moving back toward the door, walking slower than he had when he came out. His hand lands on my shoulder before he steps inside. "I'm glad you're here. Bone marrow or no bone marrow, I'm happy you're back. It's been too long since I've laid eyes on you, and I didn't want to leave this earth without ever seeing you again."

I place my hand on top of his, regretting so much of the past. "You're not going anywhere, Ian, and neither am I."

He smiles down at me, giving me a slight chin dip. "Night."

"Night, kid."

As soon as I'm alone again, my phone vibrates in my pocket, and I retrieve it, finding a message from my buddy Gil.

Gil: Deal went through. Money's in your account.

I restored an old Indian, leaving it at his shop to be sold because I didn't have time to do it before heading back here. The money from the sale will be enough for me to live on for months, without having to worry about my recovery or finding a job right away.

Me: Thanks, man. 'ppreciate it.

Gil: Let me know when you're back and need more work.

Me: Will do.

I don't have the heart to tell Gil I'm not coming back. I had my fun in California, but wherever I land after Ian is squared away, it won't be on the West Coast.

Before I turn off my phone screen, a message flashes at the top and almost knocks me off the chair.

Luna Gallo liked your post.

Rosie's twin sister. This means only one thing... the woman has talked about me. And no matter what her mouth says to my face, I've left an impression.

If I have to be trapped in this town, I may as well have a little fun. And that will include the hot little Gallo with the mouth of fire.

5

ROSIE

UNKNOWN: Hey...

I stare at the screen, waiting for something, but I don't know what. I'm scared to move, worried that any movement will cause him to extend the conversation and give him the wrong idea.

Fuckin' Luna.

She did this shit. I never would've gone to his social media and stalked him. I especially would've never liked or commented on any of his posts, drawing attention to myself.

But Luna...she always has to stir the pot.

The Queen of Drama strikes again.

Unknown: I need to postpone the tattoo for a while. I just thought you should know so you don't wait for me or think I stood you up.

I breathe a sigh of relief.

Me: No problem. No big deal at all. Thanks for letting me know.

I curse myself a little as soon as I hit send. I should've just replied with *Okay*. Too many words lead to too many thoughts and opportunities for him to reply.

Unknown: You good?

"Fuck," I hiss into the empty room, hating myself for the rookie mistake. "I'm a dumbass."

Me: Great.

Don't ask him. Do not ask him. I repeat the words inside my head as I type out.

Me: You?

My mother always taught me it wasn't polite not to reciprocate asking how someone was if they asked me the question. I hate my politeness and the manners my parents instilled in me.

Unknown: Eh, continually paying for my past and living the dream all at once.

Curling to my side, I stare at the screen, my fingers hovering over the keys, wondering if I should reply. There's not much more to say after that statement.

His past sucked. That much, I'm sure of. I watched the Walsh family from a distance when I was little, hearing nothing but hateful profanity making its way through the trees of my backyard. High school was filled with gossip and the trial of Nevin Walsh after he killed his father.

I have no doubt Nevin did it in self-defense, but somehow, he was tried and found guilty of manslaughter and sentenced to ten years in prison. If his family had had any money or pull in the county, he would've walked away scot-free. But he suffered the consequences of being poor and had his life ruined before it ever started.

The Walsh kids had shit luck being born to such a horrible father, while people like me lived a charmed life, surrounded by amazing and supportive parents along with an extended family who would help me with anything without asking any questions. The Walsh kids never had that and probably never would.

Me: Sorry.

Unknown: Don't be sorry for me. Someone has to have a shit life. Better me than you.

I wouldn't argue with him on that point. I never would've survived in his household. My sisters wouldn't have either. We definitely wouldn't have thrived and grown up to be the people we are today. My sister Gigi is a rock star mom, a caring wife, and a great big sister, even if she is in our business a little too much. And Luna…well, she's Luna, but she'd jump in front of a moving bus if it meant saving my life.

Me: No one deserves a shit life. No one should have to live one. At least you got out.

who's more put together and all glitz and glam. Her dirty-blond hair cascades over her shoulder, framing her cleavage perfectly. Her blue eyes pop with the smoky cat eye she went for, which is perfect since she's on the prowl.

"You look gorgeous…as always."

"You do too, except for the old, oversized T-shirt and leggings. I gave you a half hour, and you look like you're ready for a slumber party and not a biker bar."

I shrug. "I give no shits. I'm not here to get laid. I'm here to make sure you don't get into any trouble."

"I'm here to get into a little trouble, babe. Don't rain on my parade. You stay here and hold up the bar, and I'll live enough for the two of us."

"Sounds like a plan," I say, hating that I agreed to come here tonight. "I'll be right here, keeping the seat warm."

She touches my shoulder, moving my hair. "Smile a little. It'll make you look more approachable."

"I don't want to be approachable."

"Maybe your prince charming will be here."

I stare at her with zero amusement on my face. "You're losing time."

She pops up on her toes and kisses my cheek. "Wish me luck."

I roll my eyes. "Good luck," I mumble, but I know she doesn't need it.

The men haven't taken their eyes off her since we

walked in. Every single time someone walks by, they make comments about her "sweet ass" and "pretty lips" without even trying to be coy. They think they're the wolf and she's the prey, but with Luna, they all have it ass-backward. She knows exactly what she's doing and what she wants, and she will stop at nothing to make it happen.

But with all things Luna, she makes some missteps and gets herself into sticky situations. She does need a wingperson with her, but she needs a brother. I don't have the patience at times to deal with her bullshit or the strength to deal with the men.

She looks over the crowd, zeroing in on someone. Her posture changes, and she pushes her tits out more, even though they don't need any more attention. A second later, she's off, stalking toward her target.

"Hey, darlin'," a man mutters at my side no less than five seconds after I'm alone.

"Not interested."

"I didn't offer anything."

I turn my face toward him and glare. "I'm a lesbian," I tell him because it's the only thing men like him seem to understand and run away from faster than if his ass were on fire.

He stares at me a bit, his eyes wandering to my shirt. "Figured by your outfit, but thought it was worth a shot in case I was wrong."

"If you don't have a pussy, I'm not interested," I tell him before throwing back half of my beer.

"I can find some pussy for us if you're into a group thing."

I shake my head. "No cocks ever, buddy. Sorry, but you're wasting your time."

"Fuckin' shame. All that ass and tits for nothing."

"Yeah. Yeah," I mutter.

I can already tell tonight's going to be a long and miserable time.

6

DYLAN

"YO, FUCK OFF, MAN," I growl as the man stands next to Rosie, staring at her like she's about to become his next meal.

She freezes, her entire body tensing as soon as the words leave my mouth. She turns her head slowly, and her eyes widen for a split second as they land on my face. "What are you…"

I swing my gaze back to the asshole standing a little too close, staring at her tits and ignoring my request. "Either you're deaf or stupid, and I'm guessing the second one is right, but you have three seconds before…"

"Before what?" he replies without looking at me because he's too busy sizing up her breasts, creating fantasies that'll never come true. "Bitches like her play hard to get. It's their thing. They like—"

I don't let him get the rest of the statement out of his mouth before I thrust my arm forward, and my fist connects with his face, snapping his head back. He staggers backward, but before he loses his footing, I grab him by the shirt and yank him toward me so we're eye to eye, his nose bleeding.

"I asked you nicely, and you didn't listen. I warned you, and you still didn't fuckin' listen. I figure an asshole like you only understands a message when it's delivered with a fist. Now, you can go, or we can take this shit outside and I can finish beating your ass to a pulp, busting up the rest of your face."

"Dylan, what the…" Ian, my younger brother and the bartender in this shithole, starts to ask before we make eye contact, and his voice trails off before he finishes.

"Shut it," I tell Ian before giving my full attention back to the asswad in front of me.

The man paws at my hand, trying to break my hold, but he gets nowhere. I only tighten my grip and maintain eye contact.

"Bitch isn't worth it," he mutters, finally smartening up.

I inch closer so I can smell the stench of old beer on his breath. "Wanna rephrase that?"

"I'll go," he whispers, the fear in his eyes clear as day.

"Now, apologize."

His eyes widen. "No fuckin' way."

I raise my hand, and he cowers immediately.

"I'm sorry," he tells Rosie, but there's no sincerity in his voice.

I tilt my head, glaring at him. "Say it like you mean it."

"I'm sorry, ma'am," he repeats in a softer tone.

I release my grip on his shirt and push him away from Rosie, finally letting him stagger until he bumps into a table and finds his footing.

"You're gonna pay for this shit," he seethes, wiping his upper lip where blood had started to collect. When he drops his eyes to his hand, seeing the blood, his anger only grows as his gaze hardens. "You have no idea what you started, boy."

I let out a bitter, short laugh, not giving two fucks about the drunk asshole. I jerk forward as if I'm going after him again, and he flinches, causing my laughter to grow.

"You'll wish you never touched me!" he yells, inching backward like the coward he is.

"Fuck off!" I yell back and step toward him. "I think you need to be beat unconscious."

"Clusterfuck," Ian mutters, and even though I'm not looking at him, I have zero doubts he scrubbed his hand down his face and cursed into his palm.

The man stares at me from a safe distance and lifts his hand, giving me the middle finger before running toward the exit like his ass is on fire and the fresh air will somehow put it out.

When I turn around, Rosie's standing with her arms crossed, head cocked, and those beautiful, pouty lips flat. "Do you feel like a big man now?" she asks.

I blink, cocking my head just like her. "I'm the asshole in this somehow?"

She twists her lips. "Uh, yeah."

I scrub my hand across my forehead, trying to understand her way of thinking, but come up with nothing. "Wanna explain to me how?"

She rolls her eyes and lets out a grunt. "You hit him."

I nod. "Fuckin' A. I should have beat his ass, too. He got off easy."

"Dumbass," Ian mutters, pretending to clean the counter, but he's eavesdropping because he's a nosy fucker.

She unfolds her arms and steps toward me, looking so small and fragile yet powerful at the same time. "I had things under control." She extends her arm, finger pointed, and pokes me square in the middle of my chest. "But nooooo, you had to come in and 'be the man' and insert your fist and mouth where it wasn't asked for or needed."

"Ro…" I smile at her cuteness. So tough. So fierce. So…weak.

"No," she snaps, poking me harder. "Not every woman is in need of a rescue."

I glance down at her painted nails, unable to stop my smile from growing wider from her attempt at being scary. "And what were you going to do if he laid a finger on you? Would you have poked him to death with that black nail?"

Her eyes narrow, and her finger stays where it is. "Ever think I can throw a punch too, but I prefer to use my words like an adult?"

"Doll," I whisper, smirking at the thought of her trying to punch that asshole.

"Dick," she bites out.

I reach up, lifting her chin with my finger, and gaze into her blue eyes, which are filled with defiance and anger. "Doll," I repeat. "Why you gotta be so hard? Your job is to be soft and sweet."

She doesn't tear her eyes away from mine as she says, "I'm not weak."

"Never said you were, baby. There's a time to be hard. A time to be sweet. And when I'm around, willing to pop a guy in the face for disrespecting you, I'll be the hard one while you stay sweet. You feel me?"

Her teeth grind together, sending a vibration to my fingers. "I don't need you to be the hard one."

"Too late," I tell her, letting my gaze drop to her full lips and thinking about all the wicked things they could do that don't involve talking. My thumb moves across her skin, brushing the bottom edge of her mouth. It takes everything in me not to bend down and taste her. "Who hurt you, baby?" I whisper.

"Stop calling me that," she says, but she's done nothing to move away or break the contact between us.

She likes me. She can deny it all she wants, but a woman who claims to be as hard as her doesn't stay in my grasp, holding my eyes, and paying close attention to every word I'm speaking unless they're at least a bit interested.

"What do you want me to call you?"

"Ro," she whispers, shivering as my finger caresses her skin again.

"Ro," I repeat, loving "baby" more, but whatever makes her happy, I'll call her…for now.

She blinks at the sound of her name and clears her throat, stepping backward and out of my grasp. "Thanks for the save, but next time, I don't need it, Dylan. I'm a big girl."

Here we go…back on the hamster wheel that's Rosie Gallo's brain of independence.

"You keep saying that."

"I figure a man such as yourself needs to be told more than once before it actually sinks in."

"It's permeated, Ro, but doesn't mean I'll listen."

"Impossible," she mutters, turning her back to me to face the bar.

My eyes drift over her body, taking in the luscious curve of her ass and dip of her waist. The woman is perfect in every way. Not skinny and frail like many women, but soft and subtle…made to be touched.

"Another beer," she tells Ian with a slight chin lift.

He glances at me, and I nod.

"What the fuck was that?" she asks, her eyes moving from him to me and back to him. "Did you just ask for his approval?"

Ian's eyebrows rise for a moment, probably shocked someone challenged his ass about anything. He's not typically the type people fuck with, even women. Ian tosses a towel over his shoulder and leans over the bar, getting close to Rosie's face. "No, ma'am. Just lookin' at my asshole brother, wondering how long he's going to stick around or if he's going to get the hint and walk away. He's definitely not the best Walsh brother. He's not even in the top three. He's wasting his time with a primo piece of ass like you."

"Ian," I warn.

"Dylan." He smirks, testing my patience.

"The last thing I need is either of you archaic assholes bothering me. There isn't a Walsh brother on the planet that I'd give a piece of ass to, and that includes you—" she points at me, glaring at me over her shoulder, and then she turns back to Ian "—and you."

"Fair enough." He shrugs and pulls a beer out from the cooler, popping off the top, and setting it in front of her.

"I'll take one too," I tell him as I move next to her, not ready to call it a night or leave her alone.

Rosie lifts the bottle toward her mouth, but before she takes a sip, she glances over at me. "Maybe you should go to the other end over by the bimbos who are more your type."

I touch my chest, pretending to be offended by her statement. "Why do you assume they're my type? Maybe I like women more like you. I don't like easy."

She grunts, keeping her eyes on me as she places the rim of the bottle against her sweet lips and downs half the contents.

"I prefer a little chase in my hunt," I say just as she places the bottle back on the bar.

She wipes her lips with the back of her hand like she's one of the boys, but nothing about her screams masculinity. "All men say that, but none of them mean it. As soon as pussy's right in front of your face, you couldn't care less how you came about it as long as you get it."

"You know nothing about me."

She lets out a small laugh, and her blue eyes

sparkle in the shit lighting of the bar. "You know nothing about me either."

"We can change that," I offer, wanting nothing more than to learn everything there is to know about Rosie Gallo.

"Not on your life," she mumbles, going back to nursing her beer and ignoring me.

But I like her attention, even when it's bad. I grew up with negative bullshit and it didn't break me then, so she sure as fuck won't chase me away now.

"Baby, why so cold? You were showing that sweet side when we texted earlier. Now you're like ice."

She stares straight ahead, robbing me of her beautiful eyes. "I wasn't sweet. I was being respectful. There's a difference."

"I like when you sweetly disrespect me."

She finally turns toward me and rolls her eyes. "Listen, Dylan. It's never happening with us. You can move along to an easy target or some other prey you *may* have a chance with. I'm a Gallo. You're a Walsh. The two don't mix."

"I'm a Walsh by name only."

"Still a Walsh. Whether I think you're hot or not."

"You think I'm hot," I tell her with a smile.

"You're asinine."

"You're hot as fuck," I say, laying it out.

"I know," she replies, catching me off guard.

She has attitude and confidence. A one-two punch

that goes straight to my dick. "We could be friends, Rosie Gallo."

She stares at me, searching my face, and I'm hopeful for a hot second that she'll at least agree to be something to me. "That's a negative, buddy."

My hopes are momentarily dashed, but I've never been one to give up, especially not that easily or quickly. "You'll change your mind."

"I will not."

I scoot closer until the sides of our arms are touching and lean over until my mouth is near her ear. "You will, baby," I whisper, making my intentions crystal fucking clear.

She doesn't move for a second, and I can't see her face until she turns so her mouth is so close to mine, I can smell the beer on her breath. "No means no, in case you missed that messaging as part of civilized society."

"You'll ask me for it."

She blinks, staring at me in disbelief. "You're delusional."

Fuck, she's so damn beautiful and strong. I want to grab her face and haul those lips to mine, devouring every drop of her until she has nothing more to give.

"I'm persistent, and when I see something I want, I go after it until it's mine. And news flash, baby— right now, I'm looking at what I want to possess."

She doesn't respond right away but continues to stare at me while taking shallow, fast breaths. "You're…"

I move a little closer until our lips are touching, and I can feel the heat of her skin against my face. "Don't say something you don't mean. I'd hate to prove you wrong, Rosie."

"No one possesses me," she whispers against my lips.

My smile is immediate. "Good to know you're free."

"That's not what…"

"Shh, baby. You haven't found the right man. But don't worry, you have now."

She moves back, out from my orbit and the gravitational push and pull that flows between us. "I have to go," she says and reaches into her pocket.

"I got it," I tell her. "My girl never pays for her own drinks."

"I'm not your girl," she says, pulling out a ten and throwing it on the bar. "Never have been and never will be."

"We'll see," I reply as she narrows her eyes on me one more time before letting out a huff and stalking toward the exit like she's running from her future.

And whether she knows it or not, she is.

Nothing in my life has been easy, except women, and they grow tiring in a hurry. But there's something about Rosie Gallo that has me wanting to explore every inch of her and see what really makes her tick.

Gauntlet thrown. Challenge accepted.

"You have zero shot," my brother says from the other side of the bar as I watch Rosie's hips sway with each step.

When she finally disappears, I turn back toward him, still not liking him even if we're blood. "That girl will be mine. No doubt about that shit."

"You're a Walsh. We're not good enough for the Gallos. You know how their family feels about us."

"I haven't thought of myself as part of the family in seventeen years, Ian. I'm here only to help you and for no other reason. I'm sure as soon as you have what you need, I won't be welcomed back into the fold… not that I'd want to be anyway."

"That's bullshit, brother."

"It is what it is, and don't call me that. You haven't bothered to see if I was breathing since the day I walked out the door. Don't bother pretending to care now."

"Still an asshole."

"An asshole who's here to save your life," I reply.

He gives me a chin lift before heading back to waiting on customers and leaving me in peace to finish my beer and figure out how to win over Rosie Gallo and make her mine.

7

ROSIE

I BARELY HAVE the key in the ignition when Luna climbs in the passenger seat and slams the door. "You were going to leave me in there?"

I groan and lean forward, placing my forehead against the steering wheel. "*He* was in there."

"He who?" she asks.

I lift my head and throw my hand toward the bar. "Dylan."

She turns as if she's hoping to see him. "No shit. That's great news, yeah?"

"No, Luna, it's not. And he punched some asshole in the face."

She stares me straight in the eyes like I'm speaking a foreign language. "Did the asshole deserve it?"

"Yes, but—"

"There's no but. The guy was, in fact, an asshole,

and another guy—a very hot one, by the way—took care of him. I don't see the issue."

"I had it under control," I tell her, gripping the steering wheel so tightly my knuckles start to turn white.

"You're ridiculous. When a man's around, let him handle the dirty work. Plus, there's nothing sexier than a man who swoops in to save the day."

"Babe, you're batshit crazy."

She shrugs, totally not giving a shit what I say to her. "Never claimed to be sane, sissy."

"God, I love you, you freaking weirdo."

"You too. Now—" she adjusts herself in her seat, ticking her chin toward the road "—drive. We have a better place to be."

"Where?" I say, grinding my teeth because Luna's better places are never better places, just wilder.

"The Caves." She motions toward the street with her hand as if I'm just going to follow her directions and drive without putting up so much as a small fight.

I shake my head at her stupidity. "Absolutely not. I remember what happened the last time we went there."

"I'm not going to let one douche drugging me ruin that place forever. It's the hottest spot in the area to hang out at night, and tonight, there's a huge bash going on."

"I want to go home," I tell her because I know

there's no talking sense into her, but she'd never go without me.

"Fine," she says, crossing her arms. "Take me home, and I'll grab my car."

I jerk my head back and stare at her. "You can't go alone, dumbass."

"Either you come with me, or I'm going alone. Those are the two options. I'm not missing the biggest party of the year."

"Trust me, it's not like you'd be missing much. This isn't Vegas or New York. Drinking beer around a campfire near an old cave isn't exactly high-class or all that exciting."

"You comin' or not," she asks me with her chin raised and head tilted.

And God fucking damn...I can't let her go alone. That's my downfall. Whatever stupid shit she does, I'm always there to bear witness and watch over her as if I was somehow appointed her guardian angel because she doesn't have any common sense.

"I'll take you," I mutter as I turn on the engine and head toward the street. "But I'm not happy about it."

I have no doubt tonight will end one of two ways. Either Luna will cause trouble—it's her superpower—or I'll die of boredom...which, right about now, sounds pretty damn good.

"Shocking," she teases with a smile on her face, settling into her seat, knowing she's victorious.

And she is. That's the thing about sisters and twins. I can never let her go off half-cocked without me because if something happened to her, I don't think I could ever survive. And if I did, half of me would always be missing.

"We'll only stay an hour," she promises me, which is a lie.

"Whatever," I mumble as I head toward the Caves.

Twenty minutes later, we're parked and have beers in hand, surrounded by people who have very little life ambition besides getting shit-faced drunk and partying their asses off like it's their job. For many of them, it very well might be because they've never held down employment a day in their lives. Many of them still live at home with their parents or are looking like they're on the six-year plan to finish college...if they're lucky.

Luna's sitting on the log at my side, leaned back, showing her cleavage, and looking like the temptress she is and always has been. I'm much more buttoned-up, always struggling with my weight and not feeling right in my own skin. I wish I had her confidence, but no one has made me feel as beautiful as Luna is besides Luna and my family.

I know I'm easy on the eyes. I mean, I can see

Luna's beauty, and we have the same face. Mine is just fuller in some areas, along with my waist being thicker, my tits being bigger, and my ass definitely wider.

"There're a lot of hotties here tonight. Who do you have your eye on?" she asks me, swinging her legs from side to side with her feet firmly planted on the ground. It's as if she's sending out a signal to all the testosterone-carrying humans nearby that she's ready to mate, and man, they're taking the bait.

"None of them," I sigh. "It's slim pickings."

There are at least ten sets of eyes on us, some new and some old. But when I say "us," I mean Luna. She's the shining star. The gem every man wants to capture and add to his collection of treasure. I, on the other hand, am an afterthought.

It used to bother me, but I've grown comfortable in my invisibleness to most men. The ones who go after Luna would never be my type anyway. I have higher standards, while my sister only cares if they are hot, hard, and packing at least six inches. She doesn't set the bar too high, which makes her options vast, even in our small town.

"But how is that possible?" she asks without looking at me. "There're so many of them."

I take a sip of my beer, letting my eyes wander over the crowd that's been here for a while and is clearly not sober. "I'd rather be home with a book than here, Luna. There's no one here worth my time."

"You're going to be alone for a long time if you think like that, Ro. You have to put yourself out there. Some guys might surprise you, but you won't know that as long as you sit over here like Mother Teresa."

"When are you going to settle down?" I ask her, putting the questions on her instead of me. "Eventually, you have to date someone. The one-and-done shit has to get old after a while."

"Hasn't yet." She laughs and puts her beer down on the ground before placing her hand on my knee. "But I'll let you know when I find the one. You have to sample the goods before you buy a nonreturnable item."

"You should really stop drinking."

Using my knee as support, she pushes herself up. "I'm going to go mingle. You coming?"

I shake my head. "I'll sit here and read," I tell her, reaching for my purse.

She recoils. "You can't read here."

"I can read anywhere," I reply, digging out my phone. "It's the wonders of technology."

She places her hands on her hips, staring down at me in judgment. "If we didn't have the same face, no one would ever believe we're identical twins."

"No truer words have ever been spoken," I mutter

as I open my newest book and slide down onto the ground, using the log to support my back.

"I can stay," she offers, but I wave at her with my hand.

"I'm fine. Go," I say, preferring the company of my book to listening to her shamelessly flirt with the opposite sex. "Have fun."

"You sure?"

I raise my face to her, seeing her only in shadows, the fire roaring behind her back. "Yes, Luna. I'm sure. Your hour starts now, so you better hurry."

"Always a killjoy," she mutters as she stalks off toward a big group about thirty feet away on the opposite side of the fire.

"Hey," a man says, but I don't even look up.

"Not interested."

"Whatever," he says, getting the hint without having to be told twice. Maybe the men here aren't as stupid as many of them look.

I swipe my screen, opening the page of a new chapter of my current favorite read, and ignore the laughter and talking all around me. I'm not interested in getting drunk or hooking up with any of the locals, something I've avoided for the last decade. My sister, though…she has always been about the carefree, fun lifestyle, giving the middle finger to the patriarchy and the traditional role of women.

We were both taught to be strong and independent our entire lives, and we are and always have been, thanks to our parents. Raising three girls couldn't have been easy, but they gave us a set of skills to protect ourselves and be self-reliant, something I will always be grateful for.

"Rosie?" someone says, and I peer up at a face I haven't seen in a while.

"Hey, Petey," I reply with little enthusiasm.

"Whatcha doin'?" he asks.

Peter Walters, also known as Petey, has always been a nice guy, but he has a box of rocks inside his head, which doesn't leave any room for brain power. But I've never held that against him because whatever he doesn't have in smarts, he's made up for in kindness.

"Reading."

He smiles. "I like to read."

I smile back, trying to be cordial even though he's interrupting me. "Me too."

However, he doesn't read my body language at all and bends down, crawling next to me and making himself comfortable against the log. He leans over, trying to see my screen. "Whatcha reading?"

"A book," I answer, being cagey because my types of books are no doubt not his types.

"I like comic books," he tells me, which doesn't shock me at all. "I could stare at the pictures all day."

"That's nice," I say, going back to staring at my screen, hoping he'll get the hint.

"My favorite is Superman."

Nope. He doesn't take the hint at all. "Yeah," I mumble, but I don't look in his direction.

"I have an entire collection. You want to see it sometime?"

I glance at him out of the corner of my eye and rein in my bitchiness at his interruption. He's just being nice, and I shouldn't be an asshole because I want to read. I'm sure there isn't a person here who's being nice to Petey, and he came over to me, hoping to find a friend in the crowd.

"Maybe, Petey, but I work a lot."

"Whenever you want, Rosie. Just drop on by. I live in the same place I always have. You know where it is."

"I do," I tell him. "If I'm ever over that way, I'll drop by." In all honesty, I'm rarely over in his part of town, and even if I were, there's no way in hell I'm going to Petey's house to look at his comic book collection. It's sweet of him to offer, though. The man couldn't and wouldn't hurt a fly.

"Who's your sister talking to?" he asks me, and I peer up, following his line of sight. "Never seen him around here before."

My blood instantly runs cold. The man across from my sister has a face I'll never forget, but she certainly has by the way she's laughing and allowing him to touch her.

I stand, tucking my phone into my purse, and take a step forward. "Rosie, where ya going?" Petey asks, but I have no time to be nice and answer his question.

I stalk around the fire, my arms at my sides, my body vibrating with anger and hatred toward the man who drugged my sister years before. I'm sure that hadn't been the first time he'd done that, but she wasn't one of his victims because I was there to swoop in and rescue her before he had a chance to have his way with her without her consent.

I grab Luna's arm, and she turns her head, staring at me, confused. "Rosie, what are you—"

"Don't talk to him," I order her, shooting a look his way.

His eyes darken as he straightens his back. "Fuck off, bitch. This is between us, and you're not invited."

I tighten my fingers around her arm, and I'm hanging on by a thread. "You need to shut the fuck up, asshole."

He barks out a bitter laugh, cracking his knuckles. "Or what?"

"Hold up," Luna says, turning her deathly glare toward the man who isn't bad on the eyes and could get laid without having to drug people. Clearly, he's a psycho who gets off on the control of the unwilling and unconscious. "You do *not* get to call my sister a bitch, you cocksucker."

"Sister?" His eyes narrow as he studies my face. "I don't see it, and even if she is, she's still a bitch, sticking her nose where it doesn't belong. She came out of nowhere to interrupt what we had going, and I don't take kindly to shit like that or bitches who insert themselves where they aren't wanted. If she weren't so fat, maybe she could get some cock of her own because she clearly needs to get laid."

Luna moves forward, because the crazy bitch will always have my back, but I pull her back and slide myself between her and the man who I'm sure would've raped her tonight if given the chance. "Rosie, no," Luna says, knowing I'm going to go off and go off bad.

He moves forward like he's going to touch my sister and somehow make a move, but I move too, putting us only inches apart. I peer up, looking into the eyes of a criminal. "I know who you are and what you do," I tell him, snarling. "She won't be one of your victims. No one here will be."

"Oh my God. What? It was him?" Luna asks behind me, her fingers at my waist and digging into my muffin top. "This is the douchebag who drugged me?"

"Fucking bitches," he hisses. "Talking shit out of your asses. I didn't do fucking nothing."

"You drug women," I bark straight into his face. "I'm sure you rape them too."

He doesn't even recoil as his top lip curls. We stare at each other, a crowd around us, people murmuring to one another, no doubt thinking either I'm crazy or he is.

"Lying cunt," he snaps and leans forward, bringing his face and beer-laden breath closer. "I'm going to teach you a lesson about minding your own damn business."

"Fuck off, loser!" I yell back and quickly lift my leg, ready to knee him in the balls. But to my shock, he's expecting it, grabbing on to my thigh with one hand and backhanding me with the other.

Pain shoots across my face from my cheek to my ear, and I hear nothing but the ringing of a weird, off-key bell somewhere deep inside my head. I'm momentarily blinded by the impact, something I've never experienced before. Luna and Gigi have smacked me plenty of times in my life when we were pissed or playing, but never has a blow landed with such force to render me fucking stupid with pain.

I shake my head, trying to see straight and find my bearings, when Luna rushes forward, but she is quickly stopped by an arm around her waist. I watch in horror as she's hauled backward, and her body is replaced by a bigger one.

"You're going to pay for that one, motherfucker,"

a man says, going after the guy who just about laid me out. "You touched the wrong woman, and I'm about to make you bleed."

I try so hard to focus, but my vision is blurred and doubled. But I know the voice, having heard it less than an hour ago, warning me about how my mouth could get me into trouble if I weren't careful.

Dylan rushes forward, clocking the dickhead with an upper cut to the chin, and jumps on him as they both tumble to the ground.

"Well, fuck me," Luna whispers, watching Dylan as he beats the living hell out of the asshole for laying his hands on me. "That's hot."

"Luna," I warn because now isn't the time, and while part of me thinks it's hot, I'm embarrassed and pissed that I needed the rescue, and from none other than Dylan Walsh.

Not only am I going to have a bruise on my face, my ego won't quickly recover from this evening either.

8

DYLAN

"You. Do. Not. Put. Your. Hands. On. Women." After each word, I land another blow to the asshole on the ground as he tries to block my shots but loses.

"Walsh, you're going to kill the guy."

"Dylan, stop."

People all around me, many of whom I don't know or remember, are yelling and pawing at my back, but I'm so in the zone, they barely register.

"Dylan, please…stop!" Rosie's voice is clear as day as her face comes into focus, kneeling near the top of the guy's head before I can land another punch.

I glance up, and my gaze meets hers, conveying hurt, anger, and fear in her blue eyes.

Her fear strikes me square in the gut as hard as

the beating I've given the guy trapped under my body weight.

"Don't do this," she says, reaching out and placing her hand on my face the moment I stop the assault. "You're going to kill him."

"Good," I tell her between labored breaths, anger coursing through me like hot lava. "He deserves—"

"I know," she interrupts me. "But I think he's paid enough for now. Let the law deal with him. I mean, look at him." She waves her hand toward him.

I rest back on my heels, taking in her already-bruised face where the dickhead landed the blow.

"Look at him, Dylan. Really look," she repeats the order.

I peer down, seeing blood dripping from his nose and mouth and his face battered to the point that he won't be recognizable soon. Bastard deserves every bit of what I've given him so far and so much more. "He's looking pretty damn good to me."

She frowns and swipes her finger across my skin in a calming motion, something that's never worked on me before. "Come on. You've done enough. He'll think twice before he touches another woman."

"Men like him don't learn as long as they're breathing," I tell her, all too familiar with his type.

"Please," she begs me, sliding her hand down my arm to my wrist and giving me a slight tug. "Take me home. I need ice or something for my face."

Take her home? I know she's using it as a ruse to get me out of here and away from him, and it's working.

My eyes wander over her soft features and the discoloration that'll temporarily mar her beauty. I lift my hand, cupping her jaw gently, and slide my finger along the underside of her cheek.

She hisses, quickly biting down on her lip to stop herself from crying out at the lightest touch.

"I'm sorry, baby. He just... I just..."

"I know," she says, her eyes filled with tears, making my chest tighten and my anger start to build once more.

"Cops are coming," someone yells, and Rosie's eyes immediately widen, somehow becoming even more afraid than before.

"We have to go," she pleads, pulling on my arm harder as she tries to get me to move.

The world around us slowly comes back into focus.

The noise. The fire. The crowd.

People are scattering, running toward their vehicles, wanting to be nowhere around when the cops get here.

"Please," she begs again when I don't move right away.

I've been so consumed by my rage, I stopped thinking about anyone and anything else except making the guy bleed. But looking at Rosie's face, seeing the fear and pain that not only he put there, but I'm keeping there, has my ass up and off the ground a split second later.

I interlock our hands as we move toward the line of cars and bikes, all jammed in the same small stretch of gravel road.

Luna's with us, hustling on Rosie's other side through the darkness and chaos. "Go with him!" she yells at Rosie as our feet finally touch rock. "Meet me at home."

"What? No," Rosie replies. "I want…"

Luna and Rosie halt, but I take a few steps before my feet stop moving, and I turn to watch them.

Luna grabs on to Rosie's hands and stares at her mirrored reflection in her sister's face. "Go with him, Ro. He needs you more than me, and you need him."

I don't argue about who needs whom. There's no time. And if I'm honest, I want her with me and nowhere else. Although I don't know Luna from the next broad, she's at least talking sense.

They stare at each other for a few seconds, no more words passing between them, but they're still communicating in some weird staredown.

"Fine," Rosie finally concedes. "I'll go with him." She pushes her sister away, releasing her hands, and glances toward the horizon as it lights up in red and blue.

I don't say anything as I latch back on to Rosie's hand, hauling her ass toward my bike. Spending the night in jail isn't on my wish list for tonight. I'm not going to stick around to file a report and tell the cops why I bashed the guy's face in. With no one else here and him unconscious and bleeding, he isn't going to be talking anytime soon either.

I'll deal with the consequences later. It wouldn't be my first time getting fingerprinted and probably wouldn't be my last, but it isn't happening tonight if I can do anything about it.

We pick up the pace, making it to my bike a few seconds later, and I climb on, pulling Rosie's arm and helping her onto the back. She slides in behind me, the warmth of her body enveloping me as her thighs and arms tighten around me.

I turn the key in the ignition and give her hand a quick pat, followed by a squeeze from her before I take off, leaving a trail of dirt and gravel flying through the air where we'd once been.

I don't even know where I'm going, but I don't care. I'm only focused on getting as far away from the Caves and the cops as humanly possible while keeping Rosie safe and on the back of my bike.

She isn't fazed by my speed as everything melts away besides her body molded around mine. I don't relax until her uninjured cheek touches my back, resting against my T-shirt.

Luna pulls up beside us, motioning for me to follow her, and I do without any hesitation. It's as if I'm in a tunnel with one purpose…get Rosie home.

The only things I feel are the wind on my face and the weighted warmth of her pressed against me. The world around us ceases to exist, and nothing else matters except this moment.

In what feels like a blink of an eye, we're in their apartment, with Rosie on the couch, barely speaking and staring at the carpet as if it holds some key to the mysteries of life.

"I'll grab some ice," Luna says, looking at her sister and me, unsure of what the hell to do.

"Sit," I tell her, moving off the couch and pointing to where my ass just was. "Lemme handle it."

"But you don't…"

"Babe," I say, cocking my head. "I don't, but I will. Just sit your ass down and be with your sister. I'm sure I've nursed more bruised faces than you have. I know what I'm doing."

"Well, I…" she starts to say, but she quickly snaps her mouth shut and nods at me. She goes to the couch, sitting down next to Rosie, and takes one of her hands in hers, whispering softly.

As I flip on the light in the kitchen, I finally realize the aftermath of the ass-beating I gave the guy. My hands are covered in blood that isn't my own, and my scarred knuckles have fresh shallow cuts on them.

I smile as I remember, and I know the guy's face is in way worse shape than my hands. Making quick work, I wash my hands, removing any traces of what happened earlier besides the gashes in my skin that have already stopped bleeding.

I open their freezer and grab a bag of frozen veggies, always preferring it to straight-up ice for my wounds. When I make my way back to the living room, Luna's still whispering at Rosie's side.

Luna glances up, meeting my gaze, and I tick my head to the side, telling her as subtly as possible to get lost. Luna takes the hint, moving off the couch as soon as I kneel in front of Rosie, filling her line of sight with only me.

"Babe, I'm going to be gentle," I say softly, "but this is going to sting a little at first."

Rosie stares at me, not saying anything and not even blinking a response. When she doesn't protest, I rest one hand on her knee and lift the bag to her cheek. She winces at the contact, jerking her head back for a second before melting into the coolness.

"You good?" I ask, ignoring the cold against my palm and concentrating on her face and her facial expression.

"A little better," she whispers.

I move my thumb against her bare skin, relishing the softness and the warmth. "Good, Ro."

She closes her eyes, tilting her head to take in more of the cold. "Thank you."

"Babe, no thanks needed. We just need to keep that cheek from swelling any more than it already has. Tomorrow, you're going to have one helluva bruise too."

Her eyes snap open and widen. "Shit," she bites out like she's suddenly back to reality instead of being inside her head. "This is bad. So bad."

I give her a gentle smile, still stroking her knee softly, glad she hasn't pushed me away. "I've seen worse. It'll heal quick, and in a few days, no one will ever know."

"A few days?" she whispers and closes her eyes. "I don't have days."

"You have a hot date?" I ask, immediately regretting the question, because if she does, I'll be pissed.

"No. No. I have dinner at my grandparents', and they'll have more questions than the local sheriff during a murder investigation."

"Don't sweat it. Doctor it up with some makeup, and I'm sure they won't even notice."

Her shoulders sag. "They'll notice. I don't wear makeup often, and just the sight of it will set off their Spidey senses, and they'll know. They'll know."

She's freaking adorable in her mild panic over her family seeing a bruise on her face. Between my brothers and me, I don't think we had a time in our childhood when one of us didn't have a bruise visible on our faces. It was the norm in our family instead of the exception.

I never even knew violence wasn't part of everyday life until I left my shit-ass childhood home and traveled the country, landing with people who taught me just how fucked up my life had been.

"Cancel. Say you're sick."

Her eyes flutter open. "They'll know I'm lying."

"Better for them to know you're lying than to see the shiner you're going to have, yeah?"

She groans.

I place the veggies next to her on the couch and slide my hand along her jaw until my thumb is resting against her chin. She stares at me as I study her face, taking in the difference from each side. "It won't be that bad. I know a thing or two about this stuff, baby, and I promise no one will even know and you won't have any permanent damage."

She raises her hand, placing it against the back of mine, touching my wounds. "What the…" Her eyes move to my hand as she pulls it away from her face, taking in the cuts. "You're hurt."

I smile, loving that she cares. "I'm fine. I've had worse, and it was worth every minute."

The pads of her fingers run between the gashes. "You shouldn't have…"

I shake my head. "I wasn't going to let the man hit

you again. When I saw him raise his hand, my blood boiled over. I wasn't going to stand by like the rest of the assholes there and let him hit you again. Not happening. No way. No one's going to lay a finger on you without getting their ass beat to the point they'll think twice before touching someone else."

"That's just…" She stops, biting her bottom lip.

"Ro, baby, no one's ever going to lay another hand on you. Not as long as I'm around to make sure that shit never happens again."

"But—"

"No buts. After tonight, everyone's going to know."

"Know what?" she whispers.

"Know you're mine, and no one touches what's mine and doesn't come out looking like they've been through a war."

Her eyes widen. "I'm not yours, Dylan. Don't be ridiculous. I'm no one's and most certainly not yours." She releases my hand but doesn't move away. "I appreciate your help and the save back there, but there won't be a next time or an us."

I move her hand back to her leg with one hand and lift the frozen vegetables back to her cheek with the other. "Whatever you need to tell yourself, babe. There's fiction, and then there's reality. The reality is what it is and can't be changed. Lie to yourself all you want, but tonight made things crystal clear for everyone there, and I have no doubt word will spread quickly."

"You're ridiculous," she mutters.

"I'm living in reality, baby. Ain't no women around here I've ever put myself out for. How do you think it's going to look to all the assholes who were there tonight? They're talking and spreading that shit far and wide. Ain't no stopping the gossip train now, and if I'm being honest, I don't want it to stop either."

"But…"

I shake my head again. "I like your sassy mouth and firecracker personality. You're beautiful, and your body fits against mine like a glove. Doesn't matter what happened in the past. Doesn't matter that your dad's a dick and hates my guts. When shit works and is supposed to happen, you just gotta let it happen."

Her mouth opens and closes as her breathing intensifies. "We can't. I can't. There can't be…"

"We will, I will, and there's no stopping it," I inform her, giving her time to brace for the freight train of bullshit that's about to roll our way.

"No," she replies.

"Yes," I say.

"You should go," is her only response.

"I'm not going anywhere, Ro. I have to ice this wound and make sure you're okay."

"I'm fine," she snaps, trying to take the vegetables from my hand, but I brush her away.

"This is my job. That's part of what life is like when you're mine. I take care of you, and you let me without any lip."

"Asshole," she mumbles under her breath, and for the first time in a long time, I'm excited to see what tomorrow has to offer.

9

ROSIE

Dylan's hand moves underneath my knee, and I brace myself, stiffening my back. "What are you doing?"

He glances up, looking at me with those hauntingly green eyes and a smile that makes my belly flutter. "Carrying you to bed."

I yank his hand away from my leg, keeping a grip on his wrist, and gawk at him. "You're what?"

Is he flipping crazy? He's clearly delusional if he thinks that I'm not only *his* but that I need his help moving my body to the bed. A small sliver of me thinks it's cute and romantic, but the big part of me, the independent woman in me, thinks it's over-the-top ridiculous.

"Babe, you heard me. Not going to repeat myself."

I blink, dumbfounded by his attitude. "I can walk, and I'm not ready to go to bed."

"I know you can walk, and you're ready for bed."

I narrow my eyes, giving him my best pissed-off glare, something I've perfected over the last twenty-four years. "Uh. No."

"Baby," he whispers in a sweet and sexy voice, making parts of my body quiver when they have no right to do so. "It's easier to ice your face when you're flat on your back than sitting up."

I don't relax my face, even though he's making complete sense. Of course it would be easier, but like with most things, I don't like being told when I need to do something. And if we're going to get into the meat of it, who the hell is he to tell me to do anything? "We need to talk, and I mean really talk."

He raises an eyebrow. "About?"

"What you said before."

He tilts his head, eyebrow still raised, and stares at me. "Which part? I said a lot of shit."

"That ain't no lie," I mutter and look down when he tries to remove his wrist from my grasp, forgetting I am still holding on to him. "Sorry." I peel away my fingers, and his hand instantly lands back on my knee. I try to ignore the warmth of his skin against mine and the fact that I like his touch. "We need to talk about everything you said."

"Be more specific. I'm a man, babe. I don't

ponder every word I speak, trying to decipher hidden meanings. I say what I mean and mean what I say. And by the way, we could be having this conversation while you're lying down with your face covered in a bag of—" his eyes drop to the vegetables at my side, which have already thawed and are doing very little, if anything "—peas."

I shake my head, not wanting to get horizontal with this man in any way, shape, or form. I'm not about to give him the wrong idea, but I am about to set him on the path of what our reality is and will continue to be. "There is no us, Dylan. I don't care what happened back there or what people are going to say. There is not and never can be an us. I appreciate you stepping in, but we don't go beyond that."

"We do, though. I'm here with the peas, taking care of you." He looks so sincere when he says those words. He's being softer and sweeter than any man besides my father has ever been to me.

"Besides the fact that we'd never work, we come from opposite everythings."

He draws his eyebrows down, finally not giving me that cocky grin anymore. "Opposite everythings?"

"Totally different families. Different ways of life. Hell, we're from different decades. Nothing about us says we're a good match, even if I were looking to settle down. And I'll be honest, I sure as fuck am not looking to even go steady."

He leans back, a small laugh on his full lips, not hidden by the beard framing his jaw. "Go steady? Babe." His laugh grows louder and deeper. "You did not just use those words."

I cross my arms over my chest, growling under my breath. "I did. Shut up." Reaching out, I smack him playfully, maybe too playfully, on the shoulder. "Don't laugh at me."

"You're cute, Ro. Totally cute."

I roll my eyes. "My lot in life is to be the cute, fluffy Gallo twin who loves to eat, hates to exercise, and is the fun-killer at every party because I'm too responsible."

He stares at me, his laughter a little less, but his eyes sweep across my face and then down my figure. My body instantly heats, and red splotches no doubt cover my skin in places that are a dead giveaway that I'm feeling the weight of his gaze.

"Maybe you're a little uptight and need to loosen up and learn to have fun. And what the fuck is fluffy?" he asks, his emerald eyes back on my face.

"You know." I waggle my eyebrows, but the lines in his forehead only deepen. "Don't make me say it," I plead.

"I have brothers, Ro, and have spent the last seventeen years surrounded by men, not really having many thoughtful and long conversations with the opposite sex. Never, not once, has anyone used the term fluffy around me, not even when describing a bed or a dessert. If you're saying you're soft...a woman should be that, or at least, that's how I like mine."

I roll my eyes and scoff. "Not soft, dum-dum."

"I may not be the brightest tool in the shed, babe, but you are soft," he says while rubbing his thumb against the inside of my leg and farther away from my knee than he was before.

I shiver, unable to stop thinking about the way he's stroking me, knowing it's been for-freaking-ever since any man has laid a hand on me in a tender way. "Chunky, Dylan. I'm chunky. Luna's perfect with her small waist and flat stomach, while I'm..."

I don't get the rest of my statement out before his fingers are against my lips, stopping me. "I'm not a man who likes to be with a woman who's like a mannequin, Ro. You're soft where you should be, curves for miles, hips for days, and an ass that I could spend a lifetime enjoying without a second thought."

I swallow, liking the things he's saying, and try to keep my breathing even instead of matching the pace of my heartbeat. The man is being sweet, probably because I just got socked in the face for opening my mouth to the wrong man, a man who felt it appropriate to lay his hands on a woman.

Praise isn't something I often get, especially when

I'm with Luna. I've never felt resentment toward her about it though.

She's more dedicated and loves to work out, while I'd rather curl up with a good book than sweat my ass off. We all have our limits, and excessive amounts of sweating by running on a treadmill are over the line for me.

Our eyes are locked, his green to my blue, as my mind races with all the things to say in rebuttal to his statement. But before I can get anything out, he says, "You're absolutely perfect, Ro. I didn't even say anything about your full lips that could no doubt wrap nicely around my cock, bringing me more pleasure than I ever knew existed, or your tits, which are more than a handful, and I'd be more than happy to suffocate between at any time in my life and know I took my last breath buried in pleasure. And if your pussy…"

"Stop," I plead, feeling my core pulse, loving the dirty things he's saying, and somehow imagining his body tangled with mine. "You're sweet, Dylan. You know the right things to say, but we're oil and water. Gallos and Walshes don't mix, remember?"

"I'm sure if we shake it up enough, we would, though, babe. No doubt in my mind."

Gah. The man is impossible. I squirm, squeezing my legs together, trapping his hand. *Wrong move, Ro.*

"Thinking about all the pleasure, baby?" he whispers, his thumb stroking my skin softer and slower than before. "I'm sure you're a firecracker in the sack."

Again, I gawk at him and wonder how many women he's been with...the number has to be in the triple digits. No man looks like him and doesn't get attached without banging everything and anything that offers themselves up on a silver platter.

"I'm decent," I admit, knowing most men haven't seemed overly enthusiastic about my bedroom skills. My performance has always been described as lackluster at best, but in my defense, I haven't met a man who's had the ability to give me an orgasm. "But that's beside the point. I don't want a boyfriend, Dylan, and I'm nobody's property. You blew into town a few days ago, and I'm sure you'll blow out just as fast. Let's call a spade a spade. You're not a small-town, one-woman-only type of guy. There's reality, and then there's some fucked-up fantasy because I got hit in the face tonight. I'm not your problem, your property, or your woman."

He stands and collapses onto the couch next to me, making me almost topple over into him. Maybe my grand statement is finally getting through to him and making him look at the reality of the situation.

But before I can say anything or he does, he has his arms under and behind me, hauling me into his lap like I'm a rag doll that weighs nothing. I'm momentarily breathless and shocked by his ability and the speed at which he moved without as much as letting out a loud sigh or grunt from picking up my weight.

He continues to shift me, putting my ass on his knees and positioning me so we're face-to-face and my entire field of vision is only him. "Comfortable?" he asks, as if what he did was no big deal.

"No," I snap.

He laughs. "Well, I am," he confesses, making my belly and heart flutter in unison. He moves his hands to my waist, sliding me closer to him so our middles are touching, and there's no escaping everything that is Dylan Walsh. "I have an idea."

"Oh boy," I whisper, trying to ignore the heat of his body and the way mine responds to the hard warmth of him. It's almost maddening and makes me stupid. "I don't think I want to hear this."

He keeps one hand on my hip, moving the other to my back, stroking the sensitive skin right above my leggings. "Word's going to travel, right?"

"About?" I ask defiantly.

"About what happened tonight and what my motivation was for doing it."

I nod. "I'm sure we're the talk of the town."

Word has probably already spread through most of the population of this small town. I haven't even bothered to look at my phone, which I don't doubt is lighting up like a Christmas tree.

He smiles, and I can't stop myself from frowning.

"And just so we're clear, I don't like attention," I tell him.

"All attention or just gossip?"

"Gossip."

His fingers slide across my back underneath my shirt, flattening on the middle near my spine. "Babe, no stopping the train now. It's out of the station and moving full steam ahead. But we can control the narrative."

"And what narrative would that be?" I ask.

"You say you don't want a man, but we ran into each other a few days ago after you were on a date and the guy ditched you. So, you're not being completely honest. You want a man, just not me, which is fine. I can work with that. Minds change."

"Mine doesn't," I argue, but my body language is feeding into him and what he's saying. I can't stop myself from reacting to his touch. Small shivers, breathless sighs, and squirming every so often. I hate myself for it, too.

"Whatever you say, babe. We'll work on that." He smiles again, and my insides go all gooey. "We can just let things play out. Let people believe we're a thing. If that guy has any inkling of laying a hand on Luna or you, he'll think twice. But I'm guessing he won't dare because the ass-beating I gave him was only an appetizer."

I shake my head. "It's not good to solve things with violence."

"Women talk. Men hit. It's what we do. It's the only language we understand sometimes. It's primal."

"It's dumb."

"Whatever," he mutters. "Let people think we're a we. We'll feed it too. Go out a few times, be seen by the locals. Let them gossip, and your street cred will skyrocket."

I tilt my head and stare into the depths of his eyes. "And I want street cred because…?"

"Because every guy in this town will be after you from here on out. If they weren't thinking about banging you, they will now."

"Wonderful," I grumble. "Every woman's dream."

"You won't have to go on any more blind dates through those shit apps. You'll have the pick of the litter," he tells me as my gaze drops to his lips, unable to stop myself from staring at them.

They're full and look like they're soft and made for kissing. I'm sure they're skilled too, which only makes my body lean into him, wanting to test my theory, but I can't allow it. I place my hands flat on his chest, regretting the move as soon as I make contact

Sweet Jesus. He's rock hard underneath the T-shirt. I shouldn't be surprised by the way the material hugs his body, showing every dip and ridge. But never have I been with a man who is as hard to the touch as he is easy on the eyes.

"So," I say, but my voice cracks, and I clear my throat to cover the sound. "You want me to use you to attract other men?" My face no doubt portrays the idiocy of the entire statement I just regurgitated.

"Why not?"

"It's the worst idea ever."

He moves his hand and I close my eyes, liking the contact way too much. "You can pay me back in other ways."

I open my eyes, finding his studying my face, smirking.

"We can fool around. Maybe you have an itch I can scratch."

"No," I bite out. "I have no itches."

"You don't?" he asks, his fingertips lightly sliding up my spine. "You sure?"

I shiver at the movement, and God, I have so many itches, I don't know what to do with them all. "I'm…" I start to say.

But before I can finish the statement, Dylan leans forward, his hand flattens against my back, and he pulls me toward him. His soft, full lips land straight on mine, and I know—and so does he—I'm a big fat liar.

10

DYLAN

Rosie leans into me, wrapping her arms around my neck. She digs her fingers into my hair as her mouth opens, tasting me. The softness of her tongue and the sharpness of her nails make every hair on my body stand on end as if they're trying to get closer to her.

I slide my hand down to her ass, loving the roundness of her cheek and the perfect way it fits in my palm. Her breasts press against my chest as our bodies connect in every way that's important and possible in this position.

She moans as she kisses me deeper and harder than before, grinding against my dick with such force, I have to think about anything other than fucking her or I'll explode. I slide my hand up her back and under her T-shirt before finding the edge of her lace bra with my fingertips. She doesn't stop me but whimpers with pleasure as my fingers swipe across her nipples, finding them stiff and needy.

I groan my pleasure or maybe displeasure at the fact that we're still clothed and she's riding me like girls used to do in middle school.

Her breathing picks up as her moans grow louder, flowing from her mouth into mine. I'm getting a glimpse of the wildness in her as she rides my cock, rubbing the denim into my flesh, and I love every fucking minute of it.

She gasps and bucks as her breathing falters, and her lips clamp down on my tongue like she's trying to devour me whole. I tweak her nipple, tugging on it hard enough to send the right amount of pleasure through her, no doubt meeting the orgasm she's giving herself.

Just as suddenly as her pleasure comes, it goes. She pushes back, staring down at me with wide eyes. One hand moves to her mouth, touching her lips. "I... Um... That was..."

I smile, loving the pinkness of her cheeks and the puffiness of her lips that my body put there. "Babe, don't say anything," I tell her, dropping my hand from her breast and down onto her leg.

Her eyes don't lose their roundness as she gawks at me, her mouth opening and closing. "But I..." She shakes her head, pulling in a deep, ragged breath. "We shouldn't have..."

I raise a hand, stopping her from apologizing or making excuses. "You get what you needed?"

"Well…" She swallows as her fingertip skates across her bottom lip.

"You came, yeah?"

"Yeah," she whispers before placing her hands over her eyes, covering almost her entire face. "Oh God."

"Babe."

"Oh fuck," she hisses. "No. No. This couldn't… We couldn't…"

"We can, and you did, babe," I say and somehow hold back any hint of laughter from my voice.

She spreads her fingers, glaring at me through the cracks. "Shut up." Her body is off mine and, a second later, pacing across the floor. "That didn't happen."

I glance down at the outline of my cock, which is wet from her pleasure soaking through her leggings and onto me. "Looks like it did."

Her gaze dips, taking in what she did and left behind before she crumples over, holding her face again. "What the fuck is wrong with me?" she groans.

"Nothing, Ro. You were fucking spectacular. A real wildcat, taking what you wanted. I dig."

Her back stiffens as she stands back up, glaring at me. "You do not *dig*," she says, emphasizing the last word. "That was not fucking spectacular. That was a mistake—and an embarrassing one at that. If you tell anyone…"

I raise an eyebrow, my smug smile growing bigger. "You'll what?"

She extends her arm, pointing her finger at me. "I'll…" She huffs and pauses. "I'll…"

I move, climbing to my feet and stalking toward her, grabbing her by the back of the neck when I get close. "Baby, I don't kiss and tell. What happens here stays here, and it will every time it happens, too."

She stares at me, her teeth moving against her bottom lip before her eyes narrow. "It'll never happen again."

I let out a little laugh. "Just like you didn't have an itch, which I did, in fact, just scratch."

"You're an asshole."

"Whatever you say, wildcat." I lean over, bringing our faces an inch apart. "Lie to yourself all you want, but I know what happened, and I felt the world shift. I take back what I said before."

She blinks as her lips part, and her breathing is fast and shallow. "What you said before?"

I study her face, gazing into her blue eyes that are filled with passion and doubt. "This isn't a game to me. I'm not going to be your bait. I tasted your sweetness. Had an ounce of the goodness and softness of you. Don't want to give that up now. I'll give you time, but in the end, I know who you belong to."

"I don't belong to anyone," she says softly.

"It'll sink in soon enough. Let's get you flat on your back." The redness in her eyes has started to change, and the swelling has gotten worse in a short time.

She pushes me away with one quick blow to the chest. "I'm not letting you fuck me."

I shake my head, laughing, as she raises her chin, glaring at me. "Wildcat," I say, reaching for her.

"No." She steps back and away from me. "I appreciate your help tonight."

"With the guy or the orgasm?"

Her eyes damn near bug out of her head. She marches forward, poking me again with that finger. "You…"

I don't let her get another word out before I scoop her up, throwing her over my shoulder as she bucks and screams some bullshit, totally not understanding what's about to happen.

"Shut it, Ro," I tell her, giving her bottom a playful swat.

The door to a bedroom opens, and her twin sister pops her head out. "You good?" she asks.

I stop moving down the hallway, turning to face her. "Right as rain. Laying her down to keep ice on her face before it gets worse."

She nods. "Works for me."

"Luna," Rosie screeches, pawing at my ass. "Help me."

"Looks like you're in good hands," Luna replies, giving me a sly wink.

Her response earns her a chin lift from me before I continue to the other bedroom, which is covered in pink like a bottle of Pepto exploded inside. "Down you go," I say, placing her on the bed, missing her weight and warmth. "Keep your ass here while I get ice."

She tilts her head, scrunching her face up. "You're not going to…"

She looks so cute and innocent, sitting on the end of her bed, knees locked tightly together. Her dirty-blond hair is messy, lips puffy, face still pink from pleasure. Her tits are almost spilling out of her shirt, making me test the limits of my self-control.

"Wildcat, your face needs ice more than my cock needs pussy."

Her mouth opens and then closes as she swallows down whatever she was about to say. "Is it that bad?" she asks, lifting her hand to her cheekbone and wincing as soon as she touches her skin. "Fuck."

"I'm grabbing the carrots next and putting the peas back in. Keep your ass here."

She gives me a nod, dropping her hand back to her leg, looking defeated. "I'll be here," she whispers.

I stalk back down the hallway, finding Luna in the kitchen. "Hey," I say, moving to the freezer.

"You can go if you want. I can make sure she keeps ice on her face," she offers, leaning against the counter, watching me.

I turn, looking at her head on. "I'm good. I want to make sure she keeps ice on it all night. You good?"

She stares at me, the same blue eyes as her sister. "I'm good. Thanks for coming to her rescue...our rescue."

"Anytime, kid," I say, turning my back to her as I fish out the other bag of vegetables. "Men should never lay their hands on a woman. And if they do, they need to pay a steep price."

When I face her again, she ticks her head toward the hallway and the bedrooms. "I don't know what would've happened to her or me if you hadn't." She stops and swallows, no doubt running through all the possibilities.

"No one's going to touch either of you again. No worries, doll."

She smiles at me, looking every bit as beautiful as her sister. "You sweet on her?"

"She definitely has my attention," I say honestly and lift the bag between us. "I better get back."

"You're sweet on her," she repeats, but this time, it's not a question.

I don't answer as I stalk back down the hallway

11

ROSIE

I ROLL OVER, squinting as the sunshine hits my face, and see nothing but emptiness. I'm somehow relieved and sad at the same time. I don't know why part of me thought he'd stick around, or even why I wanted him to.

Last night got out of hand and pushed me way beyond my comfort zone. I never expected for someone to hit me or for Dylan to come to my rescue, beating the guy in my defense. I sure as hell never thought I'd end the evening being kissed by Dylan and dry humping him.

I squeeze my eyes shut again, filled with regret and shame about the last twelve hours of my life. I'm usually the one who's more reserved, and I overthink everything before I follow through. But last night, I winged it, and today, I have little doubt I'll pay the consequences.

Today, everyone will see the shiner on my face, but at least they won't know what happened afterward. At least I have one small sliver of saving grace in the debacle.

My bedroom door opens, and I hear, "Morning, wildcat."

I open my eyes, seeing a shirtless Dylan. He's holding two cups of coffee, with a bottle of pills tucked under one arm against his body, and he's smiling as if we've done this before.

"You're still here?" I ask, but the words come out a little more acidic than I wanted.

"Your face looks good," he replies, ignoring my statement and seeming unaffected since his smile never falters.

I push myself up, tucking my feet under my body, which is still covered in yesterday's clothes. "Thanks. So does yours," I tell him, holding out my hand because I need a cup of coffee more than anything else right now.

He offers it to me without hesitation. "Luna made it how you like it," he says, placing his cup on my nightstand and going to work on the bottle before retrieving two pills. "Take them. They'll help with the headache."

I take the pills from his open hand, stuffing them

into my mouth, and sip the coffee to wash them down. An awkward silence fills the room, but for once, I don't open my mouth to fill the void.

Dylan sits down next to me, studying my face as he reaches for his coffee. "It'll barely be noticeable with makeup."

"You don't know my family," I say against the mug. "They notice everything."

"From what Luna says, they already know. I'm talking about the gen pop like your customers."

"They know?" I whisper, slowly lowering the coffee mug to my leg. "Damn it."

"Guess they've been blowing up her phone." He shrugs like it's no big damn deal. "You know how word travels."

"Shit," I hiss, shaking my head. "This isn't good."

"It's not a big deal. Everyone gets a black eye at some point."

"Maybe boys do, but women do not, Dylan." I set my coffee on the nightstand where his just was. "I'm going to have to answer so many questions today."

Luna pops her head into my bedroom, holding on to the doorframe with one hand. "Have you looked at your phone? Shit is not good."

I shake my head and swallow down the lumps that are crawling up my throat. "Damn it. See?" I say, waving my arm at Dylan, "I told you."

"There's no stopping the gossip train now," Luna

adds. "Just have to hold on and brace yourself for impact. Dad isn't…"

My eyes widen and my breath catches. "Dad?" I whisper.

"He's heard, and he's not happy. Like super not happy, nearing how he was about Gigi and Pike."

"Fuck my life," I hiss, throwing myself back into the mattress and pile of pillows.

"You better get a shirt on, sparky," Luna tells Dylan. "If I know my dad, he'll be here in—"

She doesn't finish her statement when there's pounding on our front door. Not just any pounding, but a super pissed-off, you better get to the door double fast and open it up before I bust it down kind of pounding.

"Oh fuck," Luna says, her eyes widening to match mine. "He's here."

My stomach turns, and it takes all my willpower to keep the few sips of coffee from coming up. I crawl to the end of the bed and point at Dylan. "Do not move from this room."

He lifts his hands. "I won't. Your dad is an asshole and your problem, not mine."

I throw up my hands and grunt in frustration. "Since you're shirtless in my room, I'd say he'd see it otherwise if he caught sight of you," I tell him. "This is going to be hard enough. I don't need to add you to the mix."

"Dad knows Dylan was there and beat the guy silly," Luna says as my father continues to pound on the door.

"Fuckin' great," I mutter and brush past her, heading toward the door.

I don't even stop to check my face, which is a huge mistake, and I know it as soon as I open the door and my father's eyes land on me.

"I'll fucking kill him," Dad bites out, bracing himself on the doorframe like it's somehow holding him back from turning into a beast.

"He's no one, and I'm fine, Dad."

My dad's face hardens, becoming scarier. "That doesn't make it better. No one lays a hand on you. No one."

I move to the side, not wanting to air my dirty laundry for the neighbors to hear. "He's been dealt with. Trust me, he looks worse than me, and I don't think it'll ever happen again. Word's traveled all around town."

Dad looks toward the ceiling and curses under his breath before bringing his gaze back to my face. "Baby, what did I always tells you?" he asks, reaching out and gently holding my face. "Men should never lay a hand on a woman, and also, don't get your ass into situations that can lead to this."

"I know, Dad. It's just…" I don't want to finish the statement.

He doesn't know what happened to Luna a while back with the guy that caused us to show up at our cousin Mello's place with her fucked up beyond belief. I'm not about to spill the beans. I promised her I wouldn't tell, and I won't break my word now.

"The guy was messing with Luna, and I felt the need to help her. Better me than her," I say, always wanting to rescue everyone. "It's just a bruise." I try to force a smile but am immediately met by pain. "It'll heal."

My dad winces. "Baby," he whispers, his thumb sliding along my jawline. "That's more than just a bruise...it's one helluva bruise."

I lean into his touch, always finding comfort and safety in my dad. A moment later, he pulls me into his arms, hugging me tightly.

"I don't know what I would've done if..." His voice cracks.

"But it didn't, Dad," I mumble into his T-shirt as he holds me. "I'm fine."

"Fuckin' Dylan Walsh. He did me a solid saving my girls, but I still fucking hate that dirtbag loser."

The knot in my stomach twists. Dylan had to hear him, and no matter what he did in the past, he saved me. I can't think of him as a dirtbag loser, and I hate hearing my father say it too.

"Daddy," I warn, knowing Dylan can hear every word. "He was a kid when he left home. I'm sure people said that about you too at some point in your teens. It's not nice."

"Fuck nice, baby girl," he says into the top of my hair. "I had a good family to put me on the right track. The Walshes are the Walshes, and they're all the same. Trash."

I peer up at the man I've always looked up to and have done everything to put a smile on his face, unlike my sisters. "That's not true. He's a good man, Dad. Maybe the rest of his family isn't, but he is."

He raises an eyebrow. Alarm bells no doubt going off in his head because of my stupid mouth. "And you know this because?"

"He saved me, didn't he?"

"Any man would do that," he says firmly.

I shake my head. "There were lots of other men there when the guy hit me, but no one stepped in except Dylan. No one else did a damn thing. Only him. Only Dylan Walsh."

Dad releases me but immediately places his hands on my cheeks. "I'm thankful he was there to help you, but that doesn't mean he isn't an asshole, baby. Men don't always do good things for honorable reasons."

I back out of his grasp, placing my hands on my hips and tilting my head. "And what reason would he have to help me, Dad?"

He crosses his arms over his chest, lifting his chin. "You know the reason."

I mimic his movements. "I want you to say it."

Dad snarls, grumpier than normal, but not shocking with the situation. "No man does anything out of the kindness of his heart. He'll want something for it, and it's a price that's too steep to pay."

"He didn't even ask for a thank-you," I tell him.

"Yet, baby. He hasn't asked for anything yet."

"Good morning," Luna says, finally walking out from the hallway to enter the conversation. "Nice to see you."

"Mornin', baby."

Luna walks over to my father and pops up on her toes, kissing his cheek. "Stop giving Rosie a hard time, Dad. She didn't do anything wrong, and Dylan isn't like the rest of his family."

Dad stares at her and then turns his gaze on me. "You both seem to know a lot about this boy, and you're spending a lot of time defending him with having only been around him for a few minutes while he beat a man half to death."

"He stopped at the shop for a tattoo. And he's only back in town because his brother Ian has cancer, and Dylan came to find out if he can donate bone marrow to him. He's the last hope at a match in the family before they start searching elsewhere. So not only did he save Rosie, he's hoping to save his brother's life too."

"His brother has cancer?" I ask in disbelief. Dylan

134

didn't go into detail with me before, and the news rocks me to the core.

"Yeah. Ian told me about it a few weeks ago when I was at the bar. We had a long talk since the place was a ghost town. He said he didn't think Dylan would come back even for him since they hadn't talked in years, but here he is… He's a good man, Dad. So stop being such a jerk about him."

"I can still appreciate what he did for Rosie and hate him at the same time," Dad replies, being his usual difficult self.

"You're ridiculous, Dad. Are there any men you actually like?" Luna asks.

"Only those in my family."

"You didn't like Pike, and now you love him."

"He proved himself worthy."

I roll my eyes, ready to shoot off some smartass comment, when my dad's phone buzzes. He glances at his phone and curses again. "I have to go. Your mother is beside herself. If she hadn't had an appointment this morning, she'd be here next to me saying the same thing."

"I have to get ready for work. It's going to take some effort to hide this bruise."

"Not enough makeup in the world will hide it," Dad says.

"I have full-coverage stuff. No one will notice. I promise we won't embarrass you," Luna tells him.

"I'm not worried about being embarrassed, baby. Just take care of yourself." He looks at me. "You too, kid."

"We will, Daddy," Luna replies for the both of us. "You better get before Mom gets mad."

Dad mutters again and walks over to me, kissing my cheeks, and then does the same to Luna. "I love you two."

"We love you too," we say in unison.

He walks toward the door, turning around before walking out. He takes another look at my face, the rage still boiling under the surface about what happened.

As soon as the door closes, Luna and I finally let go of a very long breath we've been holding.

"Shit," she mutters.

"Yeah. That could've been a major shitshow."

"He handled it well," she tells me. "I mean, he could've seen Dylan, and that would've been a…"

"Clusterfuck," I finish her statement.

I turn, seeing a fully dressed Dylan in the hallway, leaning against the wall and out of sight from where my father had been standing. His head is down, staring at the tile floor, probably mulling over the nasty shit my father said.

"I'm sorry," I say to him as I walk across the living room to where he's standing. "He doesn't know you and has no right—"

Dylan lifts his head and hands. "Babe, he doesn't know me, but neither do you. He's right. I'm not a good man. I've done bad shit, and I feel like no matter how much good I do now, the bad will always follow me, especially in this town."

I stand directly in front of him and place my hands on his biceps, forcing his arms down. "We all do bad things, but people change. The man I saw last night had nothing but good in him."

"Your dad was right, wildcat."

"About what?" I ask, confused.

His gaze is focused on mine, his face hard and emotionless. "My reasons weren't entirely honorable. I may not have beat that guy because I wanted in your pants, but it's the only thing I've thought about."

I lift my hand to his face, brushing my fingers against the coarse hair of his beard. "I'm pretty sure what happened on the couch last night didn't help you to stop thinking that way either. It doesn't make you a bad person. If I'm being honest, I've pictured you naked more than once in the last twelve hours."

"You know you've pictured me naked since you saw me at the bar," he says, a small smile on his lips. "I saw the way you looked at me."

I smack his chest, holding my laughter. "I can neither confirm nor deny that statement."

He reaches up, touching my cheek so tenderly, my eyes instantly water. There's so much depth to his touch and so many emotions in his gaze. "Whatever this is, or could be, can't happen, wildcat. I can't let you destroy the relationship you have with your family because of me. I'm not worth it, nor am I worthy of it."

"Don't say that."

He leans forward, his lips touching my skin. "You deserve better, Ro. You're fierce, loyal, and beautiful. You deserve so much better than anything I can offer, but if you need me or need another rescue, I'll always be there," he whispers against my cheek.

"Dylan," I say softly, wanting something, but I don't know what else to say.

He drops his hand, breaking the connection. "I have to go, wildcat."

"Wait," I beg, reaching for him as he starts toward the door.

He stops walking, and I run up beside him, giving him a kiss on the cheek just as tender as the one he gave me. "Thank you," I whisper, grabbing on to his hand.

He smiles down at me, and my body warms and my belly flutters at the way he looks at me. No one has ever looked at me that way. I have never been the one to get the attention of men, especially not when Luna was around. But with Dylan, I felt like the only girl in the world, and a small part of me will miss that.

"Bye, Rosie." He walks toward the door but

doesn't let go of my hand until he's so far away, they naturally drift apart from distance.

"Bye, Dylan," I say as the door closes.

He's gone, and the knot in my stomach changes, turning to an emptiness I don't quite understand.

DYLAN

"Wait!" Rosie yells.

I peer over my shoulder, finding her running after me.

"Stop!"

I turn around as she gets closer and grab her by the shoulders before she slams into me. "What's wrong?"

"Don't go," she begs, curling her fingers into my T-shirt. "It doesn't matter what my father says. You were kind when you didn't need to be. You rescued me when you didn't have to. I've seen a glimpse of the man underneath this hard exterior, and I want to know more. I want to take you to dinner this week-end…as a thank-you."

I raise my eyebrows, taken aback by her offer, and move my hand to her beautiful face. "You don't need to do that, wildcat. You've been sweet to me, something not many people around here are. That's enough for me."

She smiles, her blue eyes sparkling in the morning sun. "You were the sweet one. Please, let me do this. I want to do this."

"You want to take me on a date?" I repeat her earlier statement, still in shock and confused as fuck.

She nods, her smiling growing wider. "Yes. Saturday night. I'll pick you up."

"Ro, I'll pick you up. We'll take the bike."

She peers around me to my bike, and her lips twist before she returns her eyes to mine. "I'm more of a car girl."

"You need to let go a little. Let your hair blow in the wind and feel the freedom of the road. You pick the place and time, and I'll be here, wildcat."

"Saturday at five."

"Five?" Who the hell goes on a date at five unless they're old as fuck?

"Yes, five. It's a bit of a drive to the place, and I don't want to show up too late."

I shrug a shoulder, still holding her face. "Whatever you want. You want five, I'll be here at five."

Her hands flatten against my shirt, sliding up my chest, and wrap around the back of my neck. "Thank you," she says softly, inching up on her tiptoes and bringing her face close to mine. "You won't regret it."

I slide my hands down her body, gripping her hips. "I have no doubt."

I fully expect her to pull away and leave, but she doesn't. She comes closer, moving her lips toward mine, her eyes searching mine for approval.

I don't wait for her to make the final move. I take control, bending my neck, placing my lips over hers, and tasting her sweetness, letting myself get lost in her softness.

She kisses me back with more hunger than she did last night. Our bodies are pressed right and perfectly together as the sounds of our breaths become one and fill with need. I wrap my arms around her, leaving no space between us, and grip the back of her neck with one hand, holding her captive in this moment.

She breaks away, breathing heavy, and stares at me like more than a kiss passed between us. "Saturday," she whispers.

"Saturday," I repeat, trying to catch my breath and get my body under control before I climb on my bike and leave. "If you change your mind, you know how to reach me."

"I won't," she says, watching me as I walk backward toward the parking lot of her apartment complex.

Part of me knows I should've said no, but I can't. Not to her. There's such a sweetness underneath all her strength which I've never experienced or seen in another woman. The way she looks at me is different too. I'm not a piece of garbage in her eyes, even though she knows all about my family and their less-than-lackluster reputation around our small town.

Even if we only get Saturday night, I'll do everything in my power to make it the best night ever, and hopefully dessert will include her.

"YOU'RE DOING WHAT NOW?" Ian asks, sitting next to me on the front porch as an afternoon thunderstorm starts to roll our way.

"You heard me."

"Rosie Gallo, though, bro? For real? I mean, the girl is hot, but she's closer to a nun than your normal type."

"You don't know my normal type," I remind him, not having spent time around each other in seventeen years.

Besides not seeing each other, he rarely called, typically only to drop bad news in my lap. My brothers know nothing about me. They wrote me off the day I left, and I guess, in a way, I wrote them off too.

I knew I had to go. I couldn't stay here with my father, or I would've ended up a drunk or, even worse, in jail. I needed to get away from the toxicity in the house, and I set out on the open road to make my own way in the world. No matter how bad shit got after I left, it was never worse than it was when I lived at home.

"That was your choice. You made the decision to leave."

"I had to leave, Ian. You know how the old man was. What other choice did I have?"

He rocks back and forth, taking a sip of the beer he's been nursing for an hour. "I remember. I lived it. You leavin' didn't make anything better either. Gave him fewer people to spread his anger out on. Shit only got worse."

"Staying was never an option."

"We always have choices. You made yours. We paid for it, too."

"Well, at least the bastard is dead now," I tell him.

"Wish it would've happened sooner," he mutters. "You stickin' around?"

I shrug. "Don't know. Didn't think I had much reason to stay and figured no one wanted me around anyway. Do you really care if I do once you get what you need?"

He doesn't answer right away. Ian stares out across the front yard at the sky, stewing in silence. "I think you've been gone long enough."

"No one wants me here, Ian. You've made it

perfectly clear you're still pissed at me for a decision I made seventeen years ago to save myself."

"It'll take some time for that wound to heal. I'm grateful you're here now when I need you most, and if this doesn't work... Well, then I'll need you here more than I ever have before."

I turn my head, studying his profile. "It'll work."

Ian leans forward, his elbows on his knees, and sighs. "Never know what's around the corner. I'm sorry I'm such a dick to you. I'm trying to get over the anger I had as a kid for you leaving me here with him...with them, but I want you here. Have you ever done something and never knew how to make the first move to correct it?"

I stretch out my legs, kicking back in my chair and thinking about his question. I live my life on my own terms, but I have a lot of regrets too. I don't know how many times I picked up the phone, wanting to talk to my brothers, but something always stopped me. Finding the right words wasn't easy, and they never came to me. Skipping the conversation and phone call entirely was easier. The longer time stretched, the more difficult it became to take the first step.

"Of course."

"Well, we're here. We're making the step. Stay as long as you like. I don't care what anyone else thinks, I want you here. I need you here. And even if you're here for that hot piece of ass, I'll take it."

"I'm not here for her," I tell Ian.

"Don't care why you stay, but it would be nice to have my brother back."

My head's spinning because not five minutes ago he wasn't as friendly or welcoming.

"You're giving me whiplash," I say.

Ian turns toward me. "I'm still pissed sometimes. All the feelings come flooding back from when you left, but then I remind myself it was what was best for you. Pop was always hardest on you since you were the oldest. You're here now, and that's all that matters."

"Okay."

"Okay?" Ian asks.

I nod before sucking down half of my beer. "I will stay for you, Ian. Maybe not forever, but at least for a long enough while that we'll know if you're okay. Maybe it'll be longer, but it's been years since I've stayed in one place for a stretch of time."

"The town is different than it used to be. It's grown. I'm sure you could find a job doing whatever it is you do. I'll hire you at the bar if you need work."

I stare at my brother, watching him as he fidgets. Sharing feelings had never been a strong suit in our family, and that was only amplified by the beatings our father gave us if we showed any that weren't "manly," which meant anger was the only acceptable emotion in his eyes.

"I'm not a bartender, man. I work with my hands. I'll see if there's a garage around here that needs a new mechanic. I have enough money saved to get by until after the surgery and a little beyond that. I'm in no hurry."

"New guy bought Tank's garage. It's pretty damn upscale now. Maybe start there. His name's Mammoth, and he seems pretty solid, except he's married to—" He stops.

"To whom?" I ask.

"Tamara Gallo," Ian mumbles.

Interesting. Do I really want to insert myself into Rosie's world even more by working for someone in her family? They'd probably kick my ass to the curb once they knew who I was.

"The family has their claws in everything, huh?"

"Not really, but this guy does work that'll blow your mind. He and Tamara work there with her cousin Nick, while the majority of the family stuck to Inked."

"Maybe I'll drop by there."

"You should. He has no idea about our family and has always been solid to me when he's come into the bar. Even Tamara doesn't give a shit about what happened when we were young. It was more of an issue between our father and Rosie's father, but it was ages ago."

Not long enough for Rosie's dad to forget all the

anger and hatred. We deserved it, though. Not only was my dad a miserable, drunk bastard, but we were all shitheads too, raised like wild animals.

Growing up without a mother made us almost feral at times. There was never an ounce of softness or love in our house. We communicated through jabs and words that cut deep, knowing it was the only language my father understood and allowed under his roof.

It wasn't until I got out into the world that I realized we were the exception and not the rule. People didn't go around acting like assholes, not even the men. There was a time for anger, but it didn't sit on your back twenty-four seven looking for a fight. The seventeen years of being away from my childhood home gave me time to grow and learn what being a man really meant.

"I'll check it out."

"You do that, and you can stay here as long as you want."

I shake my head and grimace. "Too many memories for me in this place. I've lived on my own too long to share a space with a bunch of grown men anyway."

"Suit yourself," he says with a shrug. "But the offer stands."

"While you're welcoming, the others are not," I remind Ian.

"They're all jealous pricks. You had the balls to leave when they never did. Ignore them."

"It's what I've been doing. I'm here for you, not them."

"So be it."

"I'm going for a ride," I tell him, climbing to my feet.

"But the storm," he says, looking out across the horizon.

"It's moving north. I'll be fine."

An hour later, I'm standing in front of Tank's old shop. He was a biker from back in the day and could make any piece of junk run after a little elbow grease. The shop looks nothing like it did when I was a kid. It has fresh paint, new cement, and glass doors for each of the bays.

A man walks out of the open bay, wiping the grease off his hands, looking nothing like the old man who used to own the place. This guy has long hair, covered in tattoos, and has an air about him that lets me know he doesn't like to fuck around.

"I'm looking for Mammoth," I tell him.

"Lookin' at him," he bites out, shoving the grease-covered rag into his back pocket. His eyes move to my bike behind me and then back to my face. "Need work done?"

"Lookin' for work."

His eyes move back to my bike, studying her,

passing judgment on if I'm worthy from the single glance. "You have experience?"

"Years. Been all over the country working in garages."

He takes a deep breath, sizing me up and not just my bike. "What's your name?"

"Dylan Walsh."

"Dylan Walsh," he repeats, his eyebrows knitting together. "Why do I know that name?"

I shrug. "Dunno, man. I just got back into town."

A woman walks out behind him and stares at me, placing her hand across her forehead to block out the sweltering afternoon sun. I haven't seen her in years, but knowing Mammoth is married to Tamara Gallo, I know it's her, and her beautiful features that were always striking when she was younger are now more pronounced.

"Princess, this here is Dylan," Mammoth says, sliding his arm around her waist and pulling her tight against him.

Tamara instantly smiles. "Walsh," she says with a dip of her head.

"Gallo."

"Saint now," she corrects me.

"Upgrade."

She shrugs, but her smile never fades. "What brings you around here? Wanting to know more about my cousin?"

I shove my hands into my pockets because while I do want to pick her brain, I'm not here about pussy. "Lookin' for work."

Her eyebrows rise. "Sticking around this time?"

I rock back on my heels, hating that everyone in this town still knows everything. "Thinking about it."

"Staying because of Ro?" she asks point-blank, getting right to the meat of the issue.

"Not entirely, but possibly."

"Baby," Tamara says, turning her gaze toward her husband, and it's filled with nothing but love. "Dylan's the one who beat the shit out of the guy who hit Rosie."

Mammoth makes a long, slow nod. "Thank you for that," he says to me. "Saved me the trouble of tracking him down and doing the same."

I don't respond. You're welcome doesn't seem fitting and is awkward under the circumstances.

"Why don't you come in and fill out an application, so we have your information," Tamara says, motioning for me to follow her inside.

"Sure," I mutter. It's probably useless. No matter what solid I did for Rosie, being hired by anyone inside the Gallo family will be a hard sell.

"When you're done with her, come back out and see me in the garage."

I nod and follow Tamara as she peels herself off her husband. "Will do," I reply.

Tamara doesn't say much, typing away on her phone as I follow her through the customer entrance of the shop to a small office.

"Sorry about that," she says, setting her phone on her desk as she takes a seat. "So…sit. Sit."

I do as she asks, sitting across from her, feeling completely awkward. "You don't have to do this," I tell her, sitting on the edge of the seat, ready to go. "I know how my family and yours…"

She shakes her head, holding up a hand. "Whatever shit you have with my uncle Joe doesn't run down to me or to Rosie. That's between you and him. What you did last night…" She stops and blows out a breath. "I don't know what would've happened if you hadn't been there. We owe you."

"You owe me nothing."

"We do, but we're also in need of another mechanic. We're busier than ever, and getting good workers hasn't been easy. Most of the kids these days don't know shit."

"Well, I know my shit."

Tamara tilts her head and studies me again as her phone starts to dance across the desktop as messages roll in.

I tick my head toward the vibration. "That about me?"

She smiles. "Maybe."

"That's a yes," I mutter, scrubbing a hand across my beard.

She reaches into the top drawer of her desk, pulling out a piece of paper and sliding it across to me. "Fill this out so I have your contact information. It'll be up to Mammoth after he knows a little more about your experience and skills."

I grab a pen lying nearby and start to write, but Tamara isn't going to let me do it in peace or quickly.

"So, you stayed the night last night. How'd that go?"

"You tell me," I say, filling in the old address that used to be my home but is now temporary. "I'm sure word's spread."

"She said you were sweet."

I growl and scribble a little faster.

"I like that," she says, leaning over the desk with her hands clasped in front of her. "Mammoth's a teddy bear. He can be a grumpy fucker like you, but around me, he's nothing but kind."

"I'm not grumpy," I grumble.

"Said like a grumpy fucker," she says with laughter lacing her voice.

"Ro's sweet on you, you know?"

I glance up, my pen not moving. "You sure about that? Her father…"

"Doesn't matter in the equation. You think my dad liked Mammoth? Don't be ridiculous. My father

153

wanted to murder Mammoth, especially after I went into lockdown and almost got killed."

My eyebrows shoot up. "Well…I…"

"So, yeah. It's all about your good deeds and how you treat his daughter. Gallo men can be the biggest, grumpy fuckers on the planet, but they're just being protective. Once they know they can trust you and that you'll protect their girl, you're in the fold forever."

"I think you're getting ahead of yourself."

She leans a little closer, staring me straight in the eye with no smile on her face anymore. "Am I?"

I stare back and say, "I don't know what the future holds, kid."

"No one does, old man. You could get hit by a bus on the way home tonight, but I'm asking about your intentions and feelings toward my cousin."

"I have no idea."

"Whatever you need to tell yourself," she says, her smile back on her face. "When you know, you know. You just need to come to terms with that reality and let it sink in."

"Fuckin' women," I mutter under my breath.

"You like her."

"We'll see."

"Nah, you like her," she tells me and starts to hum to herself.

I fill out the rest of the application in a hurry,

scribbling down my answers to the basic questions. "We good?" I ask after I slide it back across the desk.

"We'll see," she says with a nod.

I shake my head, cursing to myself. Well, one thing is for sure, Rosie Gallo isn't about to hide me, her father be damned.

Maybe I have a shot at her after all, and nothing about that thought makes me want to run.

ROSIE

I stare at my reflection in the mirror, regretting letting Luna do my makeup for my date tonight with Dylan.

"I look ridiculous," I say to myself as she stands off to the side, looking totally impressed with her work.

Luna fusses with my hair one more time. "You look hawt. Don't you dare take it off."

"I look like a clown," I grumble.

She rolls her eyes before she turns me toward her and holds my shoulders. "You look like a badass bitch. Your girls alone will bring any man to his knees, but add in the smoky eye and the red lips, and he'll be eating out of your hands."

"And I want that because?"

"Because it's better than you eating out of his."

"You're weird."

"I'm smart."

"He's seen me without all this. It's not like he's seeing me for the first time in his life."

"Doesn't matter. He'll be unable to keep his eyes and hands off you tonight."

"This is a thank-you dinner, Luna."

"Uh-huh." She winks. "He can thank you with some good dick."

It's my turn to roll my eyes. "I don't need good dick," I tell her before trying to pull up my top to cover my breasts that are reaching for my chin.

I'm not two steps away from her when her hand lands flat on my ass with a load thwap. "Well, you most certainly don't want bad dick either."

I rub the spot on my ass that only stings a little, but I'm going to milk it for everything it's worth. "We may be identical in looks, but after that, we're not much alike."

"We are, but you repress your inner goddess."

There's a light knock on the door, and Luna claps her hands, filled with so much freaking happiness. Me? My body's buzzing, and my palms are sweating no matter how hard I concentrate on slowing my breathing.

"I can't do this," I announce, standing near the doorway of my bedroom and looking at the hallway like it's made of lava.

Luna pushes me forward, not letting me back out now, and I hate her for it. "Oh no, you don't. You're going. You said you wanted to thank him, and you're gonna thank him."

Only a few people know about my dinner with Dylan tonight. It has been a few days since the night he rescued me, and my bruise has faded enough that full-coverage foundation made it virtually disappear. Thank God. Gigi was kept in the dark about the date for obvious reasons—that girl would snitch on me to Dad in a heartbeat. Tamara and Lily don't know either because the three of them are thick as thieves and I like to keep my secrets on the down-low, and nothing stays hidden when it comes to them.

It takes everything in me to make my legs move, my shoes feeling as if they're filled with lead. Every step takes effort and concentration, especially since Luna made me wear her highest and sexiest stilettos. If I don't fall and break my neck tonight, it will be a win…dick or no dick.

I take a deep breath, plaster a smile on my face, and open the door. My heart immediately skips a beat. Dylan Walsh isn't dressed in a T-shirt and jeans like I expected. He has on a white dress shirt, black tie, and a pair of what look like new blue jeans. He looked damn good before, but right now, standing in front of me all cleaned up, he looks fucking hot. He's even trimmed his beard, but it's not short, just tidier than before.

"Wow," I whisper, but not as quietly as I wanted.

"Wow yourself," he says, his eyes leaving my face, catching on my breasts before heading lower to my bare calves and high heels. "Damn, you're beautiful."

My cheeks heat, and I fidget for a minute, unsure of what to say. Luna has always been the one to be described as beautiful. I am the "cute one," but the way he's looking at me, I feel every bit as beautiful as Luna. "Should we go?" I say, somehow keeping my voice even.

"It's going to be an interesting ride," he replies, and my stomach flips.

Fuck. I forgot he said we were going to take his bike. I didn't think about that when I let Luna pick out my outfit, and she grabbed a ridiculously short skirt.

"I don't think I can…"

"You can," he replies with the most devilish smirk I've ever seen on a man's face. "You sure as fuck can, wildcat."

"Bye, kids. Have fun," Luna says from behind me, rubbernecking to see Dylan around my side. "Don't do anything I wouldn't do."

"That doesn't leave much off the list," I say to her, along with giving her my middle finger.

"Exactly," she replies. "Byeeee."

Dylan steps to the side, holding out his arm, and I take it, locking elbows with him. Without his help, I'm not sure I'd even make it down the sidewalk without catching a heel and making a giant fool of myself. I don't know how Luna walks around in these all the time. I prefer flats and flip-flops over high heels and wedges, but my center of gravity is different from hers.

"Tonight, I'm the luckiest son of a bitch alive," Dylan says. "Nothing like a beautiful woman, a short skirt, and the road."

I look at the ground, carefully watching where I step and trying not to pass out from nervousness. "Maybe we should take my car."

"I promise to be a complete gentleman until you ask me not to be."

I stumble, but he holds tight to my arm, keeping me upright.

"Don't worry, wildcat. I'm not expecting anything more than a good meal tonight."

"I wasn't planning anything more than that," I lie as we make it to his bike. In all reality, I like Dylan. I like him a lot and enjoy kissing him even more. I played off not wanting his "good dick," but I do. I haven't been touched the way every woman wants to be touched in so long I've almost forgotten what it feels like.

My phone rings in my purse, the theme song to

The Godfather filling the air.

"*The Godfather*?" Dylan asks. "Mafia boyfriend?"

I shake my head, fishing out my phone because I will do anything to waste time to keep from climbing on the back of his bike, including talking to my grandparents. "Grandparents. It's just a joke. We all have it as our ringtone for them."

"Never had grandparents," he admits, and my heart suddenly aches, trying to imagine what it would be like not to have them in my life.

I hit answer and speaker, letting him hear that it is, in fact, not my Mafia boyfriend. "Hey," I say with the cheery voice I usually reserve for them.

"Hey, baby. Whatcha doing?" my grandma asks.

I stare at Dylan and say, "Nothing. You?"

"Oh, you know. Doing old people shit."

Dylan laughs, his teeth sparkling through his beard.

"I don't know what that is, Gram, but I'm sure it's cool."

"Your grandpa, on the other hand, is doing dumb people shit." She sighs loudly.

"And what is dumb people shit?" I ask, but I don't know if I really want to know.

"Sal, I told you to get the hell off that ladder. You're going to fall and break something vital. I'm too young to be a widow," she chides him.

"Woman, we're older than dirt and held together

by cobwebs and Bengay," Grandpa says in the background.

I grimace and shrug at Dylan, who's still laughing at their ridiculousness. "Sorry," I whisper.

"They're great," he says, unable to stop himself from enjoying their free talking.

"Grandpa, you shouldn't be on a ladder," I say, speaking loudly because his hearing is shit at times, especially over the telephone.

"Girlie, I've been on ladders more years than you've been alive. I know what I'm doing."

My grandmother gasps and starts repeating the same prayer she says when doing the Rosary.

"Do you need help, Gram?"

"I tried calling your father and everyone else, but no one's answering. It's like they're all in bed and don't care if we die."

"You're being a little dramatic, Marie," Grandpa says to her. "You only called Joe and no one else. Maybe he was busy. Ever think of that?"

"What's more important than his own mother?"

"Maybe his wife. Maybe they were working on another baby."

"He's old and fixed."

If I could crawl into a hole right now and die, I would. Dylan's loving every moment of my mortification at the conversation my grandparents are having on the other end of the phone.

"They can still practice."

"Oh my God," I say to the sky, begging for a reprieve from the embarrassment.

"Your grandfather does need God in his life, especially when he's climbing on ladders, trying to off himself before his time."

"For fuck's sake, Marie," Grandpa grumbles. "Who the hell is going to hang this light?"

"You're hanging a light now? Why not wait until tomorrow when everyone's there?"

"You just answered your own question, baby. I need it fixed before dinner tomorrow. Can you maybe get in touch with one of my other grandchildren and have someone help us tonight?"

"We'll go," Dylan says before I can answer.

I cover the phone. "We can't go."

His eyebrows knit together. "Why?"

"We're going to dinner."

"We'll go afterward. You can't leave your grandpa to climb on the ladder, wildcat."

I stare at him, looking for any clue that he's kidding, but I see nothing. "I'm not with any of my cousins," I tell Grandma.

"She's at home by herself tonight, Sal. It's okay, baby. I'll try Mammoth or one of the other boys. Maybe someone will answer their phone."

"Tell them we're on our way," Dylan tells me, giving me the cute chin lift he does occasionally.

"Is that a man I hear?" Grandma asks, never missing anything. Her hearing is sharp, unlike my grandfather's. I swear she can hear the faint ping of a pin dropping from across a room.

"Yes, ma'am," Dylan answers.

My eyes widen, and I know there's no going back now. So much for keeping tonight a secret. "It is. I was heading to dinner with a friend, Gram, but we could stop by and help with the light."

"Dinner?" she asks, her voice filled with unmistakable shock.

"Yeah. He did me a favor, and I was thanking him."

"Well, you're in luck. I have plenty of dinner here. If he'd be willing to help with the light, I'll make sure he leaves with a full belly."

"No need to feed us, Gram. We'll stop by and then head out so you can rest."

"Don't be silly, child. Nothing gives me more pleasure than feeding my babies."

"Darling," Grandpa says, purring the nickname. "You sure about that?"

"At my age, Sal, I'm sure," she says with a hint of laughter. "Anyway, we'll be waiting. Take your time."

The line goes dead, and I stare at Dylan, blinking a few times.

"Are you crazy?" I ask him, unable to move and still holding my phone in the air.

"No, babe. They need help, and we aren't doing anything. Would you rather your grandfather hurt himself?"

I exhale a sigh. "No, but just so you know, they're a little…"

"Doesn't matter. They're your people, and from what I hear, I'm going to get along with them just fine."

"You really don't have to do this. I can call one of my cousins."

"Nonsense," Dylan says to me, climbing onto the back of his bike and motioning for me to get on behind him.

"Nothing about this is a good idea."

"Good ideas are never as much fun as bad ones." He gives me a wink.

I take a few steps closer to his bike, debating on how to climb onto the back in a ladylike way, but I come up with nothing.

"Step there—" he points down to a spot on his bike "—hands on my shoulders and hoist yourself up, Ro. You got this."

"My fucking ass," I mutter.

"Your fucking ass is sheer perfection. Now get on the back and slide that sweet pussy against me so we can get where we need to be."

"Slide my what?" I ask, my mouth suddenly dry and my stomach doing that weird dip again.

"Your sweet pussy," he repeats, his mouth turned up at one side and looking so freaking hot I want to do more than slide my body against his.

"Is that how you talk to all your women?" I ask, trying to distract him as I hoist myself up and over, giving the entire parking lot a show and full view of my underwear.

"Wildcat, I don't have any other women."

Any other women.

That statement infers that in some way I'm his woman and his only woman.

Eep!

"Slide a little closer," he says, moving on from his previous statement. "I won't bite, babe."

"Promise you'll go slow," I say, scooting forward until there's no space left between our bodies.

He turns the key and revs the engine before he says, "On the road, I'm the boss."

I wrap my arms around his waist, letting my fingertips slide against his tight, hard stomach. "So, then I'm the boss everywhere else?"

He pats my hands, and I grip him tighter, squeezing my legs together to stick to him as much as possible. "No," he bites out and takes off before I have a chance to complain and correct him.

"Fuck," I hiss as my heart flutters and my stomach plummets. I brace myself for what's about to come.

14

DYLAN

Rosie's off the bike before I have a chance to cut the engine. "You drive like a freaking madman."

I stare at the length of her, loving the way her face flushes when she's angry. "Babe, I went the speed limit, and I liked the way you held me tighter every time you got even a little bit scared."

She opens her mouth to yell and snaps it shut, glaring at me. "You scared me on purpose?"

I smile with a shrug, swinging my leg over the bike, and walk toward her. The front door opens, and Rosie's demeanor immediately changes.

"Thank goodness you're here," a woman says, stepping outside. "Come inside and cool off."

I glance over, soaking in her grandmother's presence. There's no mistaking the shared genetics between the two, and if her grandma is an indicator, Rosie will never lose her looks.

"Behave in there," Rosie warns me and starts to walk toward the house, but I grab her hand, tangling our fingers together.

She's still pissed about the ride, but after a minute, her hand relaxes and the hand-holding isn't forced.

"I'm not an animal, Ro. Your grandparents will love me."

She peers over, giving me a slow blink. "Don't mention my father's name. They adore him, and you…well, you know."

"I won't mention that he's an asshole."

Rosie squeezes my fingers tightly. "I'm serious."

"Me too."

"Wait." Her grandmother holds out a hand before we make it onto the first step. "Let me get a good look at the two of you." She smiles, her eyes wandering over her granddaughter and then moving on to me. "Damn, kids. You're both stunning. A total power couple."

"Gram, we're only friends."

Her gaze drops to our hands. "Only friends, huh?"

Rosie nods. "I need help in these heels. You know how clumsy I am."

"Mm-hmm," her grandmother mutters, giving

her a wink as we make it to the top of the steps. "Whatever lie you need to tell yourself, baby."

I hold in my laugh so as not to offend either of them. I love to annoy Rosie, but I'm not sure how far I can push things with her grandmother yet. "I'm Dylan, ma'am." I hold out my hand, waiting for her to take it when we're in front of her.

To my surprise, she doesn't take it. Instead, she steps forward, wrapping her arms around me and squeezing me tight. "We hug in this family, Dylan."

The embrace feels nicer than I could have imagined. There's a sweet gentleness to the way she touches me, resting her head just below my chest due to her height. This is something I missed out on as a child after my father was disowned by his entire family, along with us.

"Wait until Fran sees you," she tells me, peering up at me as she releases me and steps away.

"We won't have to worry about that," Rosie replies, earning a look from her grandmother and me. "She's never going to lay eyes or hands on him."

Grandma Gallo stares at her granddaughter with one eyebrow raised. "We'll talk about that later, sweetie. Now, Mr. Dylan, are you handy?"

"I'll give whatever you need my best shot, Mrs. Gallo."

"Grandma," she corrects me with the sweetest smile.

Damn it.

My heart flutters at the thought. People take their grandparents for granted and don't realize how lucky they are to have caring elders in their life. I had one person, and he was a complete and utter asshole.

"Lead the way," I say, unable to call her "Grandma."

She's not mine, but she is Rosie's, and I'm not going to let myself buy into the lie of calling her something she isn't to me.

Mrs. Gallo walks into the house, and I motion for Rosie to go in front of me, liking the view of her ass more than anything else. Especially in her high heels. She sways her hips with every step, calling to my primal need, and the memories of her riding me through my jeans come rushing back.

"Oh sweet Jesus," her grandmother mutters, hurrying to the ladder where her grandfather is perched high above the foyer tile. "Damn it, Sal. Get down." She turns to us, forcing a smile. "I've told him ten times, but men can be impatient, especially the older they get. No offense."

I give her a quick smile before rushing toward the ladder and grabbing the chandelier from his hands before either he falls or the new light does. One of them isn't going to make it down in one piece if I don't take it from his hands.

"I'm fine. I'm fine," he tells her, taking each rung

on the ladder very slowly and finally holding on to the sides with both hands.

"Grandpa, what in the hell were you thinking?" Rosie asks him before his feet even touch the floor.

He turns to her, his eyes lighting up when his gaze lands on her. "Rosie, baby, I've changed more lights than the years you've been alive. I could've handled it and survived."

"With broken bones," Rosie tells him as she wraps her arms around the old man. "I'd like you around for a while longer."

"I don't have any plans to go anywhere, doll, but based off the looks of you—" he backs away, soaking her in "—I'd say we interrupted yours."

"Nah. Nothing big," she says, smiling.

He peers over at me, holding the light, wearing the best clothes I have to my name. "No man wears a tie unless it's a date, love. You should've told us you were busy."

"It's really no problem," I tell him and move past him toward the ladder. "I can do this in a few minutes."

"You'll stay for dinner, though, right?" Rosie's grandmother asks. "No need to go to a restaurant."

"Marie," he warns her. "Let the kids go out and have fun."

"We'll stay," Rosie offers, and I'm not the least bit mad either.

I haven't had a home-cooked meal in months, and that wasn't anything more than a piece of chicken and some vegetables. Based on the smell, something a helluva lot better is cooking in this house.

"Dylan, do you like sausage and peppers?"

My stomach instantly rumbles, giving away my answer before I can say a word.

Mrs. Gallo laughs. "I make the best you'll ever have. I even have tiramisu for dessert."

"Tirami-what?" I ask as I start to climb upward, careful to hang on to the chandelier.

I take a moment to look around from my high vantage point. The house is pristine and palatial. Nothing like anything I've ever been in before. They don't have working-class money, but the big bucks. I knew Rosie's parents weren't poor like my old man, but I never thought her family was dripping with cash.

Her grandmother gasps, and I glance down, thinking I've done something wrong. "You've never had tiramisu?"

I take a deep breath and continue up until I'm within arm's reach of the hole in the ceiling. "No, ma'am."

"It's decadent. It's hard to explain, but it's like putting a spoonful of heaven in your mouth."

"She thinks everything she makes is heaven in your mouth," her husband says.

"Is it true?" I ask, balancing carefully and letting

go of the ladder so I can use both hands to hook up the new light fixture.

"Sure is," Rosie answers. "Gram makes the best of everything."

"You're more than welcome to come back for dinner tomorrow. We always have plenty of food, and it's a big spread."

"Gram!" Rosie gasps. "You can't just invite Dylan to family dinner."

"Why not?" her grandmother asks.

I concentrate on the light, letting them hash it out. All I know is I'm falling in love with her grandmother, but Rosie isn't exactly happy about the invitation for her Sunday family dinner. I don't want to get into why it isn't a good idea. Joe is her son, and I'd never say anything bad about him in front of her. I am an asshole just like him, but I know when to keep my mouth shut and when to let the shit fly.

"He's not my boyfriend, Gram," Rosie says.

"So? You've all brought friends before. What's the difference?"

This should be interesting. I keep working on the light, but I want to pay extra attention to the way Rosie answers this question.

"He doesn't get along with Dad."

I peer down, meeting her grandmother's eyes for a second. "He doesn't get along with your father, or your father doesn't get along with him?"

Here we go.

All aboard the clusterfuck train. I am about to lose that home-cooked meal of sausage and peppers along with tirami-whatever.

Damn.

"Do you know about the family living behind Mom and Dad's? The Walshes?"

"Your dad never liked that man. He was awful to his children."

Rosie glances up at me and grimaces before she says, "That's Dylan Walsh."

"Okay," Mrs. Gallo says.

"I'm not following here, kid," her grandfather adds. "He's not his old man."

"Well, Dad doesn't like Dylan either. He doesn't like anyone in the family."

"Oh lord," her grandmother mutters. "I thought I taught that boy better than that."

"Dylan left home more than fifteen years ago, but Dad still hates him. The other day, Dylan saved me from a sticky situation, and instead of being grateful, Dad had a bunch of horrible things to say about him."

I glance down, seeing her grandmother shaking her head and making a tsking sound. "Your father should be grateful that you had a man around to get you out of whatever that sticky situation was. And no man should be judged by his father."

"I wasn't the best teenager, ma'am," I add because I know I was an asshole. I had too many hormones and more anger than I knew what to do with. It took me a lot of years to move on from that bullshit and understand it wasn't my fault and I could determine my own fate.

"Grandma," she tells me again. "Family or not, it's my preference. Ma'am is for strangers."

"Yes, Grandma," I reply, the word sounding so foreign on my tongue.

"Thank you," she says with the biggest smile, and goddamn it if the simple look doesn't make me feel all the warm and fuzzy bullshit I've avoided my entire life. "Her father was something else when he was young. He forgets about his days before he settled down. I know more than a few people who thought he was an asshole too. A different type of asshole from your father, but still an asshole. Probably the same type of asshole you may be now, but that didn't mean he wasn't a good and honorable man."

I seriously love this woman. The way she can so easily throw around profanity and somehow make it sound normal coming from her lips is astounding.

"He didn't get the asshole from me," her husband says, holding up his hands. "He got that part of him from your side of the family."

Her eyes slice to her husband, and her hands

move to her hips as she drops one shoulder. "Why are you trying my patience tonight, Sal?"

He walks toward her, sliding his arm around her middle, and hauls her against him. "Darling, you never liked easy."

She stares at him, her body melting into his as they stare into each other's eyes. "You're impossible."

"You love me," he tells her, and it's not a question.

"Sometimes," she whispers.

"You love me," he repeats.

I've never seen a relationship like theirs. They've shown more love and caring toward each other in a few minutes than most men show their wives in the years I've been around them. I want what they have. I want something that endures decades.

"Almost done?" Rosie asks as I stare at her grand-parents, still balancing on the ladder with the light.

"Can you hand me the drill, Ro?"

She nods, carefully bending over to retrieve the power drill. There's a smile on her face when she hands it off to me. "Who knew you had skills."

"You have no idea," I tell her with a wink before taking the drill from her hands as she stands on her tiptoes to give it to me.

Rosie blushes and bites the corner of her lip, making my knees a little weak with all my dirty thoughts.

I push the images from my mind, knowing this

isn't the place or time to have them, and I get back to work. Within minutes, the light is secured and ready to go.

"Give it a try," I tell her grandmother, staying up near the light in case I fucked shit up.

She flips the switch and claps as the foyer fills with light. "Well done, Dylan," she says.

"What's that?" Rosie's grandfather asks, and I glance down, finding him close to her face, zeroing in on the remnants of her bruise.

"Nothing," Rosie says, turning her head.

Her grandfather gently takes her face in his hands, moving her injured side back to the light. "What happened? Who did this?"

Her grandmother walks over, gasping when she notices the purple underneath Rosie's makeup.

I hold my breath, worried they'll think somehow I was involved in putting that mark on her skin.

"That was the sticky situation Dylan rescued me from," Rosie answers, pulling her face away from his hands.

"Did a woman do that?" he asks Rosie.

Rosie shakes her head. "No, but I don't know who he was either. He was messing with Luna, and I tried to stop him."

"You're a good sister, Rosie." Her grandfather peers up at me, murder in his eyes. "I hope he looked worse than her."

"Made sure of it, sir," I say, climbing down the rungs of the ladder, thankful I'm not going to get blamed for shit I didn't do.

When my boots touch the tile, he places his hand on my shoulder, tightening his grip. "I can never thank you enough for stepping in and saving our girl."

"It was nothing."

His fingers tighten even more but not to an uncomfortable level. He's trying to keep me in place and keep my full attention. "It's not nothing. It was honorable and good. Men are pussies today. The fact that you stepped in and put him in his place speaks volumes about you as a person."

"Thank you."

"No, son, thank you," he says softly with a smile on his face.

Rosie's grandmother moves across the small space to stand next to her husband. "The least I can do is feed you, for your help tonight and for saving our baby."

My smile is easy because they're solid human beings. "I'll never turn down a meal."

Good people like Rosie don't just happen. She's a product of her environment…goodness is ingrained in her. My biggest fear is no matter how hard I try or how good I am, I'll always be a product of mine.

"Sal, get the man a beer, and I'll grab the food," Mrs. Gallo says, brushing her fingertips against her husband's cheek in a sweet and loving manner. "We're going to talk about how to handle our trouble-maker son and get him to see the man who's in front of us now and not a memory of the man he's never been."

"Sweet Jesus," Rosie mutters. "I don't think that's a good—"

Her grandmother looks over her shoulder. "You like this boy?"

I hold in my laughter. *Boy*. I'm thirty-five. I haven't been a boy in a long time, but I don't dare say anything. I assume if I ever make it to their age, everyone will look like a kid to me.

Rosie's cheeks turn a deep shade of pink as her grandmother watches her closely.

"Yeah, you like this boy," Mrs. Gallo says before turning back to me. "You don't worry about my son. In this family, I'm the boss. If I say you're good people, then you're good people. He acts all big and bad, but he's a momma's boy and will never cross me. You let me handle him, okay?"

"Okay," I say softly, ready to watch the wild ride of how Joseph "Asshole" Gallo is about to be put in his place by his momma.

I want Rosie more than anything, but watching her father get schooled by his mom makes it all that much sweeter.

"I have no doubt you're the boss, ma'am," I tell

her and earn myself a raised eyebrow and cocked head. "Grandma."

"Better." She nods and relaxes. "Come on. I don't want to burn the food. Rosie, get your man and take him to the table, and Sal, grab him a drink."

And just like that, I have an in.

15

ROSIE

THE APARTMENT IS dark when we get back from my grandparents'. Luna texted me earlier, saying she would be out for the night and that I should take full advantage of the alone time with Dylan.

Dylan's kicked off his boots and has made himself at home on my couch, watching me as I move around the kitchen and waste time. My stomach flips every time I glance his way and find him studying me with a sinful smile.

Shit. I did my best not to like the guy. I made it clear the first time I saw him at the restaurant after I was ditched that there was no place for him in my life. I backed up that story more than once, but now I'm faltering.

I haven't been able to stop thinking about the way he kissed me and the orgasm he gave me, even if I was the one riding him. He didn't make me feel stupid or ridiculous and has been nothing but kind…nothing like I expected him to be.

I pour a glass of wine, chugging it down quickly before refilling my glass and one for him. I want him, but I need a little liquid courage to stop from losing my nerve about going further than we did the other day.

"You going to keep stallin', or are you going to come over here and give me those lips, wildcat?"

I stop moving. My heart is thundering, and my breath catches in my chest. "I'm not stalling," I tell him. I shake off my nerves, grab the two glasses, and make my way toward Dylan. "I thought you'd like something to drink."

He takes the wineglasses from my hands and places them on the coffee table. My feet come out from under me, and my stomach plummets as I'm pulled forward.

Not only am I falling into him, but my heart is falling for him too. This is all happening way too fast, but I can't stop myself from feeling all the feelings he stirs inside me.

I adjust my body as if we've done this a million times instead of for just the second time. My entire field of vision fills with Dylan Walsh. Shades of blond, brown, and red cover his face and head, framing his soft lips as they turn up in satisfaction. His deep green eyes are brimming with emotion and hunger. Hunger aimed toward me, causing my belly to flutter again.

"Hi," I squeak as a dress shirt-covered muscular arm closes around me, caging me in.

"Hi," he whispers back, running a single finger down the side of my face and slowly drifting across my lips. "You good? We good?"

"Fabulous," I breathe and relax into him.

This is good. We're good. No man has ever made me feel like the floor is about to open below me, ready to swallow me whole.

Dylan does.

Never in a million years did I think I'd be on my couch about to have sex with him. I hadn't thought about him at all, in fact. He was only a passing memory from my childhood and nothing more...until now.

"Thank you for tonight." He smiles, his finger still tracing my features.

I sit perfectly still, propped in his lap, my body humming with excitement. "For what?"

"For dinner. For your grandparents. For being here and being you. For what we're about to do."

My heart skips. "What are we about to do?" I ask with a coy smile, pretending to be clueless or at least innocent.

I am neither, but I also have never been a go-getter, chasing after any man or sex.

His hand stops near my chin, his thumb pulling my bottom lip down and open. "Lots of dirty things."

"Lots?"

His lips turn up at one side, and his gaze goes to my mouth. "So many dirty things, you won't be able to look your family in the eye tomorrow."

The air inside my lungs evaporates, and my pussy pulses in anticipation.

"I felt that," he says, and my eyes widen.

"You felt what?"

"The twitch."

"The twitch?" I whisper, swallowing hard and trying not to be mortified that he felt my pussy's reply to his statement.

"Babe, your body couldn't be any more connected with mine than it is right now unless I was inside you. You do it, I feel it."

My entire body flushes with embarrassment, and to cover it, I throw myself forward until my lips crash into his, stopping him from saying anything more before I chicken out.

I glide my fingers through the thick, coarse hair of his beard as his mouth opens, slipping his tongue between my lips. A faint taste of wine mingles with his purely masculine scent, filling all my senses along with his hands roaming around my body over my clothes.

A moan slips from my lips when his palms glide across the sides of my breasts. He growls a response before he moves his hands to the hem of my shirt. My arms shoot up into the air as if it's an automatic response to the promise of what's to come.

He pulls away, our eyes locking immediately as the only sound in the air is our heavy breaths and the rapid beating of our hearts.

My shirt isn't even out of his hands when I do the same, grabbing the bottom of his T-shirt and pulling it off. I brush my fingertips over the warm, hard skin of his abdomen, sending all kinds of wonder through me. He doesn't speak, only watches me, his gaze dipping to the swells of my breasts as I lift his shirt.

I've never felt more beautiful than I do when he looks at me the way he is right now. He wants me, and the hard length of him pressed against my body leaves no doubt. I feel the hunger coming off him in waves.

I gawk at his chest and tattoos, running my fingers along the ink. He's hard everywhere I'm soft, and I want to spend hours tracing every dip and ridge of his perfectly formed stomach and pecs.

"We still good?" he asks.

I nod and don't get the words out before his mouth is back on mine, stealing my breath and another moan as he palms my breasts. The thin scraps of lace do nothing to block the heat of his skin against mine. I hum my appreciation, loving the way he touches me, both gentle and rough, a mix of sensations I've never felt with another man.

Dylan moves one hand to my hip, keeping the other on my breast, and pushes my lower half backward. Our lips never separate, but when he slides the hand that was on my hip between my legs and under my skirt, I gasp into his mouth.

His lips cover mine again as his hand slips into my panties and the skin on skin sends a shiver racing through my entire body. His fingers glide easily across my tender flesh, already wet and needy from the lightest touch and his deep, demanding kisses.

I spread my legs farther apart, wanting him to touch me deep. The roughness of his fingertips sends a jolt of pleasure from my core to my extremities as they sweep across the very spot where I've been dying to be touched.

A few passes of his fingers and I'm rocking into his palm, wanting more—and needing it too. My wishes are granted as a single digit dips into me, delivering total and utter bliss. He moans against my mouth, sending the vibration down my spine as every nerve ending inside me seems to come alive.

I slide my hand down his stomach to his crotch, unzipping the zipper on his jeans. Making quick work, I push the denim aside until his cock pops out, brushing against my fingertips as if begging to be touched. I move my hand around the shaft, rubbing the tip with my fingers. My eyes are open, his still closed, and I glance down to see his piercing flicker in the faint glow from the side table lamp.

Holy moly.

Piercings aren't new to me. I work at a tattoo and piercing shop, but never have I been with a man who's had his cock decorated. I've heard it's a whole new experience, and it looks like tonight I'm about to find out if the gossip is true.

He groans as I trace the metal before sliding my palm around the head to stroke his shaft.

"Fuck," he moans against my lips.

I smile, pleased with myself at bringing him as much pleasure as he's giving me. His finger leaves me, and before I have a chance to whine at the emptiness, he adds a second digit, filling me so decadently, I almost cry out his name.

He thrusts his fingers into me, and I stroke faster, trying to match his pace. I'm so close to orgasm, my toes start to curl, but before the sensation I'm craving fills me, he flips me onto my back and covers me with his body.

I flatten my hands on his back, my nails digging into his skin as his mouth blazes a path down my jaw to my neck, then lands on my breast. I arch my back, wanting the warmth and wetness against my skin. His teeth find the perfect spot, pulling at my nipple through the lace.

The delicious bite of the material and the edges

of his teeth, along with his fingers thrusting in and out of me, sends me spiraling over the edge. I moan, my body going rigid with pleasure, unable to move or breathe, only feel.

And I feel it all as he doesn't let up, but doubles down, causing my body to convulse and for me to completely lose control. Before I have a chance to come back to my senses, Dylan's mouth is off my breasts, traveling down my midsection. He flips my skirt up, placing his mouth over my clit, and sucks so hard, I instantly spiral into another orgasm, or maybe it's still part of the first. I'm half unconscious, delirious, and seeing stars when he climbs to his feet and pushes his jeans down his body.

All I can do is lie there, soaking in the beautiful muscular build of his body, the stiff, long, and more than ample width of his cock, along with the piercing that sparkles as if it's calling to me like a beacon on a distant shore.

He bends down, rustling in his pocket and pulling out his wallet, fishing out a condom. I watch in awe as he uses his teeth, the same ones that were on my nipple minutes ago, and tears open the foil packaging.

"Still good?" he asks, rolling the latex over his cock without having to look.

He's had practice, doing this probably hundreds of times with just as many women.

Don't think about that. No man is single at his age

and has a list shorter than the number of fingers on his hands. It's ridiculous for me to even think that. Whatever he did before me doesn't matter. The only thing that's important is this moment, this feeling.

"Still good," I whisper, barely able to speak but somehow forcing the words out between gasping for air.

My gaze is glued to him, mesmerized by the way his muscles move under his skin. I've never seen a man more handsome in my entire life and never one in person, standing totally naked.

Before he can settle on the couch, I stand and shimmy out of my skirt, remove my undies, and toss my bra to the side. My eyes drift lower, and I lick my lips. "Shame," I say softly. "I wanted to taste you."

"The night is young, wildcat," he replies with a wink.

I hurl myself at Dylan, smashing my tits and lips against him, excited about what the rest of the night will bring.

Dylan cups my ass, lifting me up with little effort and turning just before he hits the wall. The hardness of the unforgiving drywall pinches, but all is forgotten as soon as Dylan pushes his hard length inside me, filling me until I can't breathe.

His lips find mine, kissing me hard, taking what he wants from my mouth along with the rest of my body. I tangle my fingers in his hair, holding on as he pounds into me, angling upward and hitting all the right spots.

He grunts with each thrust, and I moan in response, our breaths becoming one, the sound of our skin slapping against each other. Tomorrow, I'll have a bruise on my back to match the one healing on my face, but this one will be worth it.

Dylan pulls away, staring me straight in the eye as he pounds into me. "You like that?"

"Yes!" I yell out, using his hair as an anchor while my tits bounce wildly.

I could give a shit what else is jiggling on my body. With Dylan, I don't care about anything except the way he makes me feel and the pleasure his body can deliver.

He lifts me higher against the wall, one hand moving from my ass to my throat, pinning my body upright. My eyes widen, and for a minute, I panic before I realize he isn't squeezing or applying pressure but is instead holding me captive as he pummels into me over and over again. He stares into my eyes with each punch of his cock into my pussy, and I can't look away.

I'm transfixed by his gaze, the way he's holding my neck, and how he spears me with his cock until I'm panting and beside myself in ecstasy.

My mouth opens and closes, words failing me as a third orgasm builds in my core, splintering throughout my entire body like a jolt of electricity. The world ceases to exist as I feel my eyes roll back, and the air sticks in my lungs.

He grunts, driving into me faster and harder until he follows me over the cliff of bliss. A few moments later, his hand leaves my neck, and he carries me backward toward the couch before collapsing with me landing on top of him.

I realize in that moment, I miss the weight of his body pushing mine against the wall. I miss the feel of his fingers wrapped around my neck.

And in this very second, I know nothing will ever be the same.

"Jesus," he mutters, dragging his index finger down my spine. "I thought you were going to kill me."

I push back the hair that's stuck to my face from the multiple orgasms. "You thought I'd kill you? Excuse me. You're the one who…"

He smiles up at me, brushing back the hair on the other side of my face. "Wildcat, I haven't fucked someone like that in forever. I wasn't sure if my heart or legs would give out before I'd be able to give you another orgasm, but I wasn't going to stop until it happened or I died."

I place my palm on his chest, lifting my head up higher to look at him better. "You didn't have to give me another orgasm."

"I don't have to do anything, but I wanted to give you another orgasm."

"Why?" I ask with a yawn.

"Because I don't want you to ever forget I was here."

"Why would I forget?"

His smile softens as he stares at me in the soft light. "Don't know, babe, but I want to make sure it never happens."

Too tired to hold myself up, I place my cheek against his chest and let my body relax on top of him. "I could never forget this."

"Me either, wildcat. Me either," he whispers, running his fingers through my hair.

"I like you, Dylan," I say, half asleep.

"Go to sleep, Rosie," he replies, and I do…quickly.

16

DYLAN

I OPEN MY EYES, blinking in confusion at the pink walls and soft blankets draped over my body. Looking to my side, I see Rosie lying next to me with her back to me, covered by only a thin sheet.

"Damn," I say under my breath as the memories of last night come rushing back to me.

The way she smelled. The way she felt. The way she cried my name. Everything about Rosie Gallo is perfection personified.

A girl like her deserves someone better than an asshole like me. I'm not worthy of a creature so pure and sweet. I've lived some bad shit, and no matter how hard I try, it never rubs off, and no number of good deeds will change that fact either.

She moves and the sheet shifts, exposing her back. I grimace, feeling a fire deep in my belly as I lock my eyes on her back. It's covered in bruises. Marks I put there from the wall and the way I fucked her without giving two shits if I was hurting her in the process.

And I did hurt her. Even though there was pleasure, marks like that don't come without a price. I know bruises. I've been hit more times in my life than I care to remember, blocking out every time my father used his fist as punishment unlike other parents.

A knot forms in my stomach at the very sight of what I've done to her. No matter what she says, I know she'll feel that for days. I can't be here. I can't stay. When she wakes up, I should be gone, sparing her the goodbyes and niceties of the morning after.

She promised me a dinner and a thank-you, and I gave her more than she bargained for. I roll off the bed, grabbing my clothes from the floor, and quickly get dressed. I move quietly, careful not to wake her, and I look back one last time, memorizing the outline of her body and the dip of her hips against the mattress.

"Perfection," I whisper to myself before slipping out of her bedroom, suddenly feeling as if I can't breathe.

As soon as I'm outside the apartment, I turn my face up into the sunshine and take a deep breath, moving toward my bike at double speed.

She deserves more. She deserves better.

I keep repeating those words, forcing myself

forward until I'm on my bike and on the road, leaving Rosie Gallo where she belongs…in the past.

***

"You're a dumbass."

I glare at Ian over my pint of beer. "No shit, genius. I never should've slept with her."

He leans over, one elbow on the bar, towel over his shoulder. "That's not why you're a dumbass."

I drink down half the glass before taking a breath and putting the scowl back on my face. "Care to explain, brother?"

"You're a dumbass because you ran away like a giant pansy."

I growl as I put my boots on the rungs of the stool, trying not to launch my body over the counter at him. "It wasn't because I'm a pansy, asshole. She deserves better."

"Better than what?"

"Better than someone as damaged as me—or you, for that matter. We're all fucked up. Dad did a number on us, and a woman like her doesn't deserve to have that kind of shit in her life."

Ian reaches up, extends his arm, and smacks me in the face, shocking me. "I'm not Dad, and you're not Dad. After all these years, you're still going to let him fuck up your life? The man's buried, and that's where you should leave the shit he did to us too. Like I said, you're a dumbass."

"Did you fucking hit me?" I ask, my brows furrowed and blinking in confusion.

"Yeah, man. But did you hear what I said to you?"

"I can't believe you fucking hit me."

"Keep doing and saying stupid shit, and I'll do it again, but harder next time."

I raise an eyebrow. "You want a black eye?"

"Wouldn't be my first," he says with a shrug. "Sure it won't be my last. And would you really hit a guy with cancer?" He gives me a pouty face and puppy-dog eyes, knowing right where to stick his dagger.

"Asshole," I mutter because he knows my answer.

"See, you're not the bad guy you make yourself out to be."

"Shut up."

He gives me a smug grin. "Was the girl mad at you after you fucked her?"

"No, and her name is Rosie."

"Whatever." He rolls his eyes, pushing back his strawberry-blond hair that had fallen over his fore-head. "Did she complain when you were giving her those bruises by fucking her silly?"

"No," I growl again.

"You ever leave marks on any other women?"

"Of course. Some women like it rougher than

others. You know how it goes. Sometimes shit gets out of control."

He dips his chin, tilting his head to the side. "Out of control like last night."

I don't respond, but I stew in my own bullshit instead.

"Shit happens, brother, but you fucked up, running out of there with your dick in your hand and not so much as a goodbye."

"Fuck," I groan, going back to my beer instead of talking to my brother and his cocky, know-it-all attitude.

"I know Rosie from the bar. She comes in here with her sister and cousins sometimes. I listen to their conversations. She's a good one. She's sweet and not as wild as the others. She may be too good for you… I take that back, she *is* too good for you, but that wasn't your call to make. It should've been hers."

A hand clamps down on my shoulder, giving me a squeeze. "Hey," a mildly familiar voice says as I turn, taking in the man from the auto shop.

Shit. He's Rosie's cousin by marriage, not by blood, but still her cousin.

"Heyyy," I say, drawing out the word and ignoring the sinking feeling deep in the pit of my stomach. "What the hell are you doing here?"

"Hey, Ian." The guy tips his chin toward my brother. "Beer, please."

"Mammoth," Ian greets him before reaching under the bar and retrieving a bottle from the cooler.

I stare at him for a minute, remembering it's Sunday and there's a family dinner I was invited to that started hours ago.

Mammoth isn't looking at me as he takes the beer from the bar top as soon as my brother sets it down. The silence is thick, and the air around me changes.

"So…" he says but doesn't go any further.

Fuck my life.

"So," I repeat before sipping my beer, trying to do something…anything instead of talking to him.

He turns slowly on the stool, the beer in his hand, staring at my profile. "Anything you want to say to me?"

"Nope," I say against the rim of my glass and not looking him in the eye.

"You sure?" he asks.

"Yep," I snap.

"Then why is there a woman sitting by her grandmother's pool crying her eyes out right now?"

"I don't know, man."

"You don't know?"

"I don't know," I repeat.

"Pansy," Ian mutters.

"You look at your phone all day?"

I shake my head.

"Give me one good reason why I shouldn't knock your ass off that stool right now."

I turn, looking him in the eye, man-to-man. "She's better off without me."

"Don't disagree with that." His eyes narrow. "But you sleep with her and leave her without as much as a goodbye like she's a piece of a road ass?"

I flex my fingers around the beer glass, grinding my teeth as I stare back at him. "She's not road ass. That's the thing. She deserves better than I can offer. Tell me I'm wrong."

He lifts his chin with a slight nod. "Can't disagree, but she should've been part of that decision-making process. Shit," he mutters, shaking his head. "'Thanks for the fuck' along with a goodbye would've been a nice touch, at least."

"How many women did you thank?" I ask him, putting him on the spot.

I don't give two shits about pissing him off more. He's already mad enough, and whatever chance I had at getting a job at his shop exploded the moment I walked out Rosie's door. I have nothing to lose now.

"Not the point. We're not talking about women in general. We're talking about a Gallo. I don't care how you treat anyone else, but Rosie's different."

"We done?" I ask him, throwing his glare right back at him. "Shit's in the past. Better that I hurt her feelings now than put her through so much more pain in the future."

"You're a real dipshit," he mutters, slamming his beer on top of the bar as he climbs to his feet. "No one who's with a Gallo is worthy of them in the beginning, not even me. But that's the thing about them. They make you want to be better...do better. And they can give a fuck what you did in your past. It's the present and future that matter. You threw away what could've been the best thing in your life."

"Thanks for the pep talk," I tell him, turning back around on my stool to face the line of liquor bottles behind the bar. "I think you have somewhere you're supposed to be."

He leans over, shadowing me in darkness. "If you don't go to her and beg for her forgiveness and love, this is one mistake that'll haunt you forever—more than anything that has followed you from your past."

"Whatever," I mumble, lifting my beer to my lips and pretending his words don't have an impact. "Duly noted."

"Dumb fuck," Mammoth mutters before stalking off.

"Well, way to piss off the entire clan," Ian says, putting himself in my line of sight. "That man doesn't say much, but when he does..." Ian shakes his head. "He's protective of the women in that family. Hell, all the men are. You're lucky you still have your teeth in that pretty little face of yours after that talk."

I shrug. "What's done is done, and no amount of intimidation is going to change that."

"He wasn't intimidating you. He was clueing you the fuck in and trying to make you realize the enormity of the mistake you're making."

"What the fuck do you care?" I snap, pushing my beer forward and tossing some bills next to the glass. "Get the fuck out of here with the fake bullshit that you give a damn what happens in my life."

"Dylan," Ian calls as I stalk toward the exit. "Wait."

But I don't.

My feet never stop moving until I'm on my bike, hitting the open road and leaving everything behind. I don't need the hassle from my brother or a stranger. What I do in my life is my decision and no one else's.

I was only looking for a good time, but things got personal in a hurry. Rosie's grandparents are as kind as she is, and I have no doubt the rest of the family is too, even her father, who I always thought was an asshole.

She deserves a guy who knows what family means and how to behave. He clearly isn't me and never can be.

My brothers and I practically grew up feral, and while I learned manners and respect after I left home,

I still don't have the knowledge to pull from not to let the shit from my childhood bleed in.

I've never had to worry about anyone else except myself. I've never worried about who I hurt or how they felt. I've worried about myself and myself alone. But with Rosie, I want to keep her safe, and that would require keeping her as far away from me as possible, even if I want her goodness in my life more than anything. I'd sacrifice my wants for her needs any day, no matter the pain I inflict on myself in the process.

ROSIE

"How'd it go?" Tamara asks Mammoth, her husband, as he stalks back onto the lanai after taking off.

"Message was delivered." He sits down, grabs her hand, and kisses the top of it. "Ball's in his court."

"What message?" I ask, looking between them as the lump in my throat rises. "And who is he?"

"No one, baby," Tamara answers, but she doesn't do it while meeting my eyes like she normally would.

"Who did you go talk to?" I ask again, and this time, my voice is louder.

"You know where I went," Mammoth tells me, and unlike his wife, he stares at me, and there's emotion gleaming in his eyes.

I gasp. "You did not go talk to Dylan." I cover my

face, shaking my head. "Oh God. Please tell me you did not go talk to him."

"Fucker hurt you," Mammoth growls. "Of course I went to have a few words with him. I ain't going to sit by and…"

I move my hands off my face and hold one up to him. "One, it's not your business."

"Became mine when you were out here crying."

I glare at him, the knot in my stomach turning into rage. "That doesn't make it your problem. Ever hear of fuckin' listening?"

Tamara laughs, covering her face to hide her amusement, but I'm not sure if it's at my statement or his clear inability not to take his own action. "Not his strongest skill," she says. "I'm sorry, Ro. He's protective."

I point a finger at her, waving it around, before I push back my chair. "He can be protective of you. You're his woman. I'm not *his* woman. I'm a cousin."

I climb to my feet, looking at everyone sitting in the circle. "I don't sit out here, spilling my guts and sharing my feelings, for people to take matters into their own hands. Every damn stubborn man in this family needs to stop. We're not helpless creatures. We aren't frail and in need of your protection. Our dads —and moms, for that matter—taught us how to take care of ourselves. We don't need men to march away to save the day every time something a little shitty happens to us. I didn't see any of you grabbing your sword and shield when the last guy broke my heart."

"Sword and shield?" Pike, my brother-in-law, asks my sister Gigi because he's confused.

Shocker. God, I love the men my cousins and sister married, but damn, they are a clueless bunch sometimes.

"She's talking about white knight shit," Gigi explains. "You all do it."

"God," I groan, lifting my face toward the sky for a moment before looking around the table. "Just because you have a dick between your legs doesn't mean you're the savior of all womankind. Stick to worrying about your own women, and leave the rest of us alone."

"Rosie," Mammoth says, and his voice is sweet when he says my name. That's the thing about Mammoth. He's one of the nicest guys you'll ever meet, but if you didn't know him, you'd probably shit your pants if he were heading your way. "Come on now."

"Come on now?" I ask, tilting my head and blinking. "Want to expound upon that, Shakespeare?"

"You're like a little sister to me."

"If I were your little sister, I would've socked you in the eye for doing that shit."

"Fuckin' women," he mutters next, not alleviating my anger at all. "You want the fairy tale, which always includes a guy who saves you and looks out for you, but then when you get it—"

Tamara smacks his arm. "Pick your words carefully."

He grumbles and swings his gaze back my way. "I'm sorry."

"Thank you," I snap. "From now on, my love life is off-limits. If I share, I share, but that doesn't give any of you the right to talk to someone as if you're my keeper. Got it?"

They look shell-shocked but slowly nod.

"Good." I collapse back into my chair, exhausted from last night and this entire conversation. I forget about my back and wince as soon as my spine meets the hard patio furniture.

"You hurt?" Gigi asks, missing nothing.

"I'm fine."

"They did it against the wall," Luna says, to my absolute horror. "You know how that feels." She winks at Gigi, giggling.

"Oh lord," Pike mutters.

"I really don't want to hear this," my cousin Nick mumbles into his palm.

"I knew you slept with him, but girl, I need more details," Jo, Nick's wife, says with a smile.

"Not now." I slide my sunglasses back over my eyes.

"Dinner's ready," Mom yells from the sliding glass doors.

"Not a word of this to anyone," I warn them.

"Lips are sealed," Lily promises. "No one will say anything. Your love life isn't anyone's business."

"It's not love," I say a little too quickly. "My sex life isn't anyone's business. That's a hard limit for me."

"Got it," Rebel, my cousin Rocco's wife, adds. "You know your secret is safe with us."

Luna pops up from her chair, and I grab her by the wrist. "That includes you too."

"Sissy," she says with a sugary bullshit smile. "I won't say anything in front of the old folks."

"In front of anyone. If I want people to know I got banged against a wall, I'll be the one to tell them."

"I'd be shouting that shit from the rooftops." She winks.

"That's the difference between us. Promise me, Luna," I say, waiting with her wrist in my hand and tapping my foot.

"I promise," she replies, sounding sad that she can't torture me for the next few hours in front of the entire family, and pulls away from me.

"Don't trust her," my cousin Trace says, standing behind me. "I know she's your sister, but she's trouble, Ro."

I turn to face Trace. "I've known her my entire

life, honey. If she keeps her promise, I'll be shocked, but it'll keep a lid on her mouth for a little while."

He throws his arm around my shoulder, moving me toward the house. "Siblings are a pain in the ass, but you'll get her back someday."

"Hopefully," I mumble as we step inside.

The house is abuzz with life. Everybody's here like they are every Sunday for dinner. The kitchen has bowls of food covering every inch of counter space. As the family gets bigger, the amount of food it takes to feed the army grows too.

There's no longer enough room around one table or even two. People are scattered everywhere with plates in their hands, wolfing down the food my grandmother and aunts spent all afternoon preparing.

I get in line before filling my plate with a little bit of everything. My stomach rumbles, hunger suddenly taking over my every thought.

I'm about to walk outside when my father catches my eye and ticks his head the way he always does when he wants us to go to him.

I blow out a breath and quickly smile, trying to cover any vibe he may pick up. He's pretty clued-in on his kids, and it's never been easy to get anything by him. He always catches Luna in her bullshit, but then, he expects it from her.

"Hi, Daddy," I say, folding my legs and sitting on

the floor by the couch he's currently using as his dinner space.

"Hey, sweetie. How's your weekend been?" he asks between bites of his lasagna.

I stuff my mouth full of pasta and make a humming noise along with giving a thumbs-up as I chew slowly.

"Do anything fun last night?" he asks, staring down at me, but his face is unreadable.

I almost choke, but somehow, I keep chewing without stopping.

Fuck.

I'm an idiot.

He knows.

I know he knows.

Stupid. Stupid. Stupid.

Of course, he knows.

I'm sure it was the talk of the afternoon how Dylan and I came here last night and had dinner with my grandparents.

Why would I think that would stay a secret? My family works one way, and secrets aren't part of the special sauce.

I swallow what feels like a softball before I answer him. "No," I lie, something I rarely do to my father unless it's for Luna's sake.

He raises an eyebrow. "No?"

"No."

"No?"

"Dad," I warn, losing patience.

"Did you do anything boring yet?"

I glance upward, meeting his questioning gaze. "Daddy, you want to just come out and ask whatever you want to ask? You clearly have a specific question. You always used to say, 'I never ask a question unless I know the answer to it.'"

He gives me a small smile. "You always did listen to every word I said."

"I may not have always followed your advice, but I paid close attention. So, be straight with me."

He sets his plate down on the table next to the couch. Luckily, the rest of the family is busy eating and talking, not paying us any mind. "Did you bring Dylan here last night?"

"Well, you obviously know the answer."

I hate when he's like this. I already know he's going to lay into me much like he did at my apartment about how Dylan's trash because his father was an abusive jerk.

Dad sighs and leans forward, placing his elbows on his knees. He moves his face closer to me in case anyone else is listening. "I'm not happy."

"Shocking," I whisper. "Grandma and Grandpa liked him and were happy he was here."

"I heard. I heard way too much about how great he is. I'm still not happy."

I set my plate down next to his and turn my body around so I'm facing him dead on. "I don't think you'll ever find happiness when it involves Dylan Walsh."

"I'm fine with him, just not when he's around my family."

My brows furrow, and I grind my teeth, thinking of the right words to say. I'm not a little girl, and although my father's approval would be nice, it's not required. "Did every parent love you when they met you?"

"No," he growls.

"Did you get into some trouble when you were young?"

"Yes." His upper lip curls because he knows where I'm going, and he hates every minute of it.

"Are you the same man you used to be?"

"No," he grumbles.

"Are you the same as Grandpa?"

"You know I'm not."

"What did Dylan ever personally do to you?"

"Nothing. But his father…"

I raise an eyebrow, twisting my lips.

"Fuck."

"He's a good man. He saved me when I could've very well gotten more than a bruise on my face. That other man had no issue hitting me once, and he could've done worse. And when Grandma and

Grandpa needed help and we were supposed to go on a date, Dylan didn't hesitate coming here to help them instead of going out."

"You deserve better."

"I'm sure a lot of people told Mom that too."

"I don't think I was worthy of your mother, but no one would've ever loved her more or treated her better than I do."

I can't believe I'm defending Dylan after what he did last night, but I can't stop myself. I'm sure it was part of his decision when he dipped out before I woke up. How could there be anything more than what we had when my dad has been against him because of the sins of his father?

"Dylan was just a kid. His father was cruel and hurt those boys. You heard him. I know I did, and I was just a little girl. He had a horrible childhood, and you're still punishing him for something he had no power or control to change. When does he have to stop paying for being born into the wrong family?"

Dad's quiet as he stares at me, taking in everything I have to say. "You're not wrong."

"I never thought I was, but thanks for the affirmation."

"I did feel bad for those boys. I called Child Protective Services more than once over how they were being treated and cared for, but somehow, he was able to keep those boys and put them through hell."

"Dylan is not his father, Dad. He's been sweet, kind, and caring when it comes to me and was nothing by respectful yesterday when he was here. I can't imagine what his life is like, except for six brothers who hold a grudge against him because he got out when they never did."

Dad reaches out and brushes my hair off my shoulder. "You're right, sweetheart."

I blink, not having expected that response. I thought he'd put up a little more fight. "I am?"

"Yes. I'm able to admit when I'm wrong."

"It's not something you've done often."

"Well, that's because I'm not often wrong," he mutters.

I roll my eyes. "Liar."

"I should be more understanding when it comes to Dylan. I don't really know the boy."

"He's thirty-five, Dad. He's hardly a boy."

"That's another thing. He's way too old for you."

"Dad." I sigh, holding my head in my hands. "You're so difficult."

"He's more than a decade older than you."

"Do you think I want a young guy who is more interested in playing video games than spending time with me?"

"No, but I'd prefer someone under the age of thirty-five."

"Well, it's a good thing you don't have to date him." I smile, giving my dad a playful wink.

He mutters a slew of curse words under his breath.

"Honey," Mom says, coming to sit next to Dad, catching all the vibes between us. "Everything okay?" The question is directed toward me.

"Perfectly fine, Mom. Just talking to Dad about Dylan."

She turns to him, studying his face. "You okay, big guy?"

"Yeah," he mutters. "Rosie's right about Dylan. I've been a shithead to a kid who was a victim and treating him like he was his father."

My mother's eyebrows rise because, again, Dad rarely says he's wrong. "He was always a nice boy to me. His father, on the other hand…"

"What do you think about their age difference? Doesn't it bother you?" he asks her.

I don't have the heart to tell them that Dylan's no longer in the picture, preferring to ditch me without a goodbye.

"You're older than me," Mom replies, grabbing my father's hand. "And we work great."

"We're different."

She jerks her head back, brows furrowed. "We

are?'"

"Yeah."

Mom runs her thumb along the top of Dad's hand. "We had nothing in common. Absolutely nothing. You were older but not wiser. On paper, we never should've worked, but here we are…happy as can be."

"We've had our issues," he says.

"All couples do, Joe. I don't care who Rosie dates as long as she loves him. Whatever issue you have with the guy, you can give your opinion, and then it's out of your hands. Don't you dare drive away our daughter because no one will ever be good enough for your baby in your eyes. You got me?"

He nods. "Loud and clear."

"Your parents like him a lot. I know your mom already had a talk with you about him. She set you straight?"

"Yes," he growls.

She gives his hand a squeeze before releasing it. "Then it's done. What's in the past is in the past."

"I owe the kid an apology for being an asshole."

I giggle. I can't stop myself from laughing when he calls himself an asshole. It's what Dylan always calls my father, and in his eyes, he hasn't been wrong. I've never truly disliked anyone, but I'm sure if they treated me shitty for something I didn't even do, I'd call them an asshole all the time too.

I somehow stop myself when my father tilts his

head, not finding my amusement all that funny. "Dylan's a lot like you, Daddy," I say between bursts of laughter.

"Another reason you shouldn't be with him."

"Joseph," Mom warns him with a stern look which isn't all that scary in anyone's eyes, especially my father's.

"What?" he asks.

She reaches over him, taking his plate off the side table and handing it to him. "Eat your food and let our baby be happy."

I smile at my mom, loving her so much. I was blessed to be born into this family with such great and loving parents. I could've had the unfortunate luck to become part of a fractured, fucked-up family like Dylan's.

"I only want her to be happy. I support her whatever she wants," he says, finally going back to his lasagna.

I'd feel the warm fuzzies if Dylan and I had any shot, but he ran away, chipping away at a piece of my heart. We ended before we started, leaving me with only a handful of great memories.

DYLAN

"The oncologist will call you when the results come in. Should only be a few days," the woman says as she unties the tourniquet around my arm.

"Thank you." I smile, waiting for her to put on the Band-Aid so I can get the hell out of here.

I don't have an aversion to needles. My tattoos are a testament to that, but I hate all things medical. I wouldn't do this shit for anyone else. Going under the knife, even for minor surgery, is not something I think I'd ever do willingly, but if this will save my brother's life, I'll put aside my fears.

"You're welcome," she tells me as I get up from the chair.

I don't stick around, walking through the crowded waiting room, and head outside. I'm almost to my bike when I hear "Dylan!" being yelled from across the parking lot.

I look in the direction my name came from and see Grandma and Grandpa Gallo walking my way with their arms hooked together.

"Hey," I greet them, tucking my hands in my front pockets as they get closer. "How are you?"

Mrs. Gallo reaches out and places her hand on my arm. "We're well, sweetie. How are you?" She looks toward the clinic. "Why are you here? Are you okay?"

It's sweet that they care. I've never had anyone who gave a shit about me besides my brothers, and even their love was surface level at best.

"I'm fine," I reply, relaxing a little bit. Obviously, they aren't holding what happened with Rosie against me. "I'm having my bone marrow or whatever it is tested."

"Who's sick?" she asks and is genuinely concerned.

"My brother. It's why I came back to town. I'm his last hope within the family for a match."

"That's very honorable, son," Mr. Gallo tells me.

"I don't know about honor, but he called and needed me, so I came."

"Not everyone would," he replies.

That shit's the truth. My father wouldn't have if he were alive. He'd let us die before doing anything that wouldn't benefit himself in some way.

She shuffles a little closer but doesn't let go of my arm. "You didn't come to dinner on Sunday. Rosie said you weren't feeling well, and then seeing you here..." Her hand tightens on my arm, and I can see the worry on her face.

"I'm fine, ma'am. I promise. I was busy taking care of my brother," I lie. "I'm sorry I missed what I can only assume was an amazing meal."

"Anytime you're hungry, stop over for a bite. I always have something on hand, and you will forever be welcome in our home."

"Thank you. You're too kind."

"Come with Rosie this weekend," Mr. Gallo says to me with such a kind smile.

I rock back on my heels, not sure how to break the news to them. "We're not seeing each other anymore."

Mrs. Gallo's face instantly loses its lightness. "What? Why?"

"She didn't say anything." Mr. Gallo looks at his wife with his eyebrows pulled down toward the center. "Did she say anything to you?"

"No," she whispers. "Not a thing, but I did have a talk with her father about being kind. No one said a word."

"It was a decision we made pretty quick."

"But why?" she asks again. "You two looked so happy together."

"She's too good for me. Rosie deserves better."

Mr. Gallo moves closer, placing his hand on my shoulder. "No man is good enough for any woman, but they make us better. Marie deserved better than me, but it didn't stop me from pursuing her. I knew I could one day be worthy of her love if given the chance."

"Sweetie," Mrs. Gallo says, both of them still touching me. "It's not only your decision to make. Did you ask Rosie what she wanted, or did you do the typical male thing and make the decision for both of you?"

I swallow, hating what I did and how I did it. "I made the decision myself."

Mrs. Gallo shakes her head. "Men," she mutters. "All these years and still not the brightest when it comes to women and love."

"Maybe I'd be smarter if I had you two in my life instead of…"

She shakes her head. "My boys had us in their lives, and they weren't much smarter. Environment doesn't always change one's perception or thought process. This is something you have to work through. And son, just because your father was one way doesn't mean you'll be the same."

My stomach sinks. "You know about my dad?"

Mr. Gallo nods. "I met him a few times, and none

of the exchanges were kind or cordial. You are not the same man as him."

"But what if I am?" I fidget, but he only tightens his hold on my shoulder.

"The man I see in front of me is kind, caring, and self-aware. You are not what you were born into. Just like I'm not what I was born into. When I was younger, I was a total shithead."

"You can say that again," Mrs. Gallo whispers, giving me a cute little smile.

"If I hadn't met this beauty, only God knows where I'd be right now."

"Jail," she adds, giving me a playful wink. "Definitely jail with your brother."

"She isn't wrong," he says, nodding a few times. "I was on my way there, growing up on the streets of Chicago back in the day. But then I met her, and everything changed."

"Sweetie," Mrs. Gallo says to me and waits until I look at her before she continues. "Your father ruined your childhood. Don't let him steal your future too."

I thought I'd left him behind when I left this town, seeing his face in my side mirrors. But I have been carrying around what he did and how he made me feel, letting it fuck with my head ever since. I'm not him. I have a temper, but every person does, and the only time I use my fists is to protect myself or those around me. I have been a good man, at least better than most, which is more than I can say about my old man.

I cover her hand with my own. "Thank you."

"For what?" she asks.

"For your kindness and wisdom. Your family has no idea how lucky they are to have you both in their lives."

"Yes, they do," Mr. Gallo says, smiling. "I make sure to remind them often."

"Salvatore."

"Come on, Marie. Let's go. We're already late, and this place is always ridiculously overcrowded. I think Dylan has some thinking to do about what he wants and how he's going to get it."

"Promise me you'll be at this Sunday's family dinner," she asks before she moves away.

"If Rosie will allow me, I'll be there, ma'am."

"Grandma," she corrects me and finally releases her grip on my arm, "And if I know my Rosie, you'll be there."

I rub the back of my neck, not as sure as she is. I have some major groveling to do. "I will do my best, but it's her decision."

"It's always their decision. Remember that, and life will be so much easier," Mr. Gallo says, leading his wife toward the front entrance to the clinic.

I stand there, watching the two of them as they walk arm in arm, looking very much in love even after so many years together. I wish I'd had that in my life, someone to show me a healthy and loving relationship. I had nothing to go on, but I am thankful for the words they spoke to me. Besides Rosie, they are the only people in this small town who seem to care about what happened to me in the past and are concerned about my future.

Before I can climb on my bike, my phone rings and my brother Finn's name flashes on the screen. I'm tempted to ignore him because he's a dick, but something makes me answer.

"Dylan, Ian's being rushed to County. I found him on the floor in his bathroom. Meet us there," he says, speaking so fast I barely comprehend what he's saying.

"Fuck. On my way," I tell him before disconnecting the call, jamming the phone in my back pocket, and heading straight for the hospital.

I rush into the emergency room, parking my bike illegally because I don't give a shit, and find my brothers in the waiting room.

"Any news?" I ask as soon as they spot me.

Finn shakes his head before going back to pacing across the small space.

Quinn, another one who isn't a fan of mine, gives me a hard glare from across the room and grunts like, somehow, this is my fault.

"They said they'd be out as soon as they know

anything," Sean says, but he doesn't look at me when he speaks.

"This is bullshit," Callum, the brother most like my father with his nuclear temper, grinds out. "They should tell us something."

"Maybe if you'd gone to medical school instead of spending your life at the bottom of a bottle of tequila, you'd be a little more helpful," Quinn tells him.

"Fuck off," Callum snaps.

"Has this ever happened before?" I ask, clueless at everything that's been happening the last seventeen years.

"You'd know if you'd been around," Finn is quick to reply, throwing the guilt of my absence right in my face.

I deserve it. I left them all behind, but they could've gotten out too. And after I left, no one reached out to me to make a new life for themselves. They were right where they wanted to be, and I was where I needed to be to keep my sanity.

"Don't be a dick," Quinn tells him, pointing a finger at my brother. "You've always been jealous he left, but that doesn't mean you can keep holding a grudge because you were too much of a pussy to follow in his footsteps." Quinn shifts his gaze my way and sighs. "It's happened one other time. It's how they found the cancer in the first place, but since then, he seemed to be doing as well as he could be with poison still inside his body."

"The family of Ian Walsh," a woman in scrubs says as soon as she enters the waiting room.

All of us turn to her and stand. "We're his brothers."

Her eyes widen for a moment as she takes in the motley crew. "He's awake and talking now. We have him on fluids. His vitals are good, but we're running some blood tests and sending him for a scan soon to determine if there's a more serious issue."

"You're aware of his cancer, right?" Quinn asks.

"Yes, sir. We're aware. As soon as he's back from the scan, you can see him, but only one at a time. When we know more, I'll be sure to let you know."

"Thank you, Nurse," Quinn tells her, looking relieved.

"Dr. Baker," she corrects him, and he rocks back like he's been kicked in the gut.

"Sorry. Thank you, Doctor."

She gives him a nod and does another sweep of us. "Any other questions or concerns before I get back to him?"

"Can we take him home today?" Finn asks because he's a dumbass.

"It's highly doubtful. We'll probably keep him overnight for observation, especially with his cancer diagnosis, but we'll know more in a couple hours when we get some of the test results back."

"Thank you for the update, ma'am," I tell her with a dip of my chin.

She doesn't stick around to have more dumb shit hurled at her by my brothers.

"Well," Callum says, collapsing into a chair and kicking back. "I'm off today. I can stick around."

"I'll stay too," I offer.

"You don't have to," Quinn tells me. "It's not like you've been around before."

I point to the bandage on my arm. "I went for my blood test this morning. If I didn't want to be here, I wouldn't. I have as much right to be here as any of you. If you want to be pissed at someone, be pissed at yourself that you stayed as long as you did. I offered to take each and every one of you with me, but you made your choices just like I made mine."

Quinn and Finn grumble under their breath, calling me more than a few names.

Sean, the quietest of my brothers, stares at the bandage on my arm like it holds the secrets of the universe. "So, we'll know in a few days if you're a match or not. If you're not…"

"I will be," I promise him, but I have no clue. "What are the odds that none of us are a match? They said twenty-five percent chance any of us would be a match to him, and since none of you are, I have to be. I just have to be."

I take a seat across from my brothers, preferring not to sit next to them, and think about all the things I could've done differently. The list is short. Sticking around would've landed me in a bad place, probably prison or knocking up someone and repeating the pattern my father set.

The only regret I have is the disconnect I have with my brothers. After seeing Rosie with her family, I want a little sliver of that for myself. We should be closer than we are. Only time will heal the wounds our father inflicted and we let widen through time and distance. And for that to happen, I'd need to stick around.

I now have two reasons to stay in this small-ass town. Rosie Gallo and my family. If I can win her back, grovel at her feet and beg for forgiveness, the rest will come over time. Without her, I don't know if I can stay here, seeing her beautiful face everywhere, reminding me of what I could've had if I'd had the smarts to realize I wasn't my old man.

"Well, you can do what you need to do to help him and then go back to wherever you've been," Finn says. "No need to stick around."

"I'm not leaving," I tell him and all of them. "I'm back, and I'm not leaving. We have shit to straighten out. Shit the old man robbed us of, and I'm not going anywhere until we figure out how to do that."

"We'll see," Quinn adds. "Sometimes it's easier to run than stick it out."

I turn to him with a curled lip. "Do you want a medal for being a martyr and staying with the asshole? You think you're better than me because you took his abuse year after year, waiting for the fucker to die?"

Quinn growls and crosses his arms, stewing in his own self-loathing and pure hatred for me.

Sean leans forward, resting his arms on his legs. "Time hasn't healed some wounds, Dylan. But we're thankful you're here, even if you only came back for Ian."

"I came for Ian, but I'm staying for the rest of you."

Callum turns toward me, brushing his dirty-blond hair back with his fingers. "Where have you been, by the way?"

"Everywhere and anywhere."

"Jail?" Quinn asks.

I shake my head. "I did join the service, did four years overseas. Saw some action in the Middle East, but that was ten years ago."

"Huh," Quinn mutters. "Never knew you enlisted."

"Didn't feel the need to share." I shrug. "Thought

I'd make a career out of it, but four years was enough of following orders for me."

"And after that?" Callum asks.

"As soon as my boots touched American soil, I bought a bike and took off, letting the wind and road take me wherever it wanted. I've been to every state except Hawaii and Alaska on the back of my girl."

"Can't say I'm not jealous," Sean says. "If I could do it all again, I'd enlist. Maybe see more of everything on Uncle Sam's buck."

"You're not too old. You can still join up," I tell him.

His face scrunches up. "I'll think about it," he says, but I know he's full of shit. Everyone's good at talking a big game, but following through is something entirely different.

"It's not as great as it sounds," I inform him, wanting him to know the reality and not the glamorized version they sell to young kids. "Asking permission to take a shit is next level."

"Yeah, I'm good," he replies, holding up his hands. "I couldn't make it through boot camp anyway. I'm not in good enough shape."

"What are we going to do if you're not a match for Ian?" Quinn asks, switching topics as he rubs the back of his neck.

"Whatever happens, we'll figure it out as a family," Finn says, and he speaks those words looking right at me. "All seven of us."

I let out a deep breath I've been holding. For the first time in years, my brothers are including me, and I have a brief glimmer of hope that things could work out...at least with my family.

ROSIE

I WALK in and sit down next to my sister, joining my cousins at the bar to get out for a night. It was their idea, not mine. They wanted to get my mind off what happened with Dylan, and I came along, but not without dragging my feet.

"So, don't get mad," Gigi says, and I already know I'm not going to like it.

Nothing good starts with that statement. Nothing.

I let out a deep sigh before giving her my full attention. "What?"

She ticks her head toward the bar, and my eyes meet Dylan's.

I slink down in my seat, feeling like a fool. "What's he doing here?"

Luna shrugs. "He's filling in for Ian, which is weird."

I sit up again, fidgeting with the waiting beer bottle. "What happened to Ian?" I ask.

"He collapsed earlier today and is at County for the night," Luna replies.

"And you know all this because…" I wait for her to answer me, tapping my foot feverishly under the table.

Luna rubs her forehead, avoiding my gaze. "Because I ordered the beer and made small talk with him."

I groan. "Why would you make small talk with him?"

"He started it. He asked about you first."

My back stiffens. "What did you say?"

Luna rolls her eyes before she answers. "I said you were great. Totally played it off like everything was fine and you weren't the pitiful mess that you actually are."

I lift my chin, hating to be a victim. "Good. I'm perfectly fine without him."

"Whatever you need to tell yourself, babe," Tamara adds after my grand statement. "I heard you were bitchy at work all day today, and you're never bitchy. There's only one person to blame for that, and he's standing over there looking all tall and handsome."

"Hey now," Mammoth says to his wife, sliding his arm around the back of her chair and resting his hand on her shoulder. "You have someone tall, dark, and handsome right next to you."

She smiles at him and gives him a kiss. "I only have eyes for you, baby."

"Better only have eyes for me, princess, or I ain't doing something right."

"You do everything right."

Luna pretends to gag. "You two seriously make us ill."

"Speak for yourself," Lily says with a goofy smile. "They're adorable. You're just jealous."

"Oh yeah. I'm so jealous about sleeping with the same man for the rest of my life," Luna tells Lily, rolling her eyes the entire time.

"That's because you haven't slept with the right one," Gigi says, putting her in her place. "Once you do, you'll stop looking for your next."

"Never happening," Luna mutters. "I'm too young to settle down. So much peen, so little time."

An awkward silence falls over the table. The men are mortified, and the women are holding in their laughter at the ridiculousness of my sister.

"Someday, you'll grow up," Nick tells her, shaking his head, judging her.

Luna grabs her beer, raising it in the air. "Not anytime soon. I have too much life to live before I'm tied down."

Mammoth grunts again, something he does well

and sounds so sexy when he does it, too. "You really need to be tied down and taught some restraint," he tells her.

I almost fall off my chair, but somehow, I stay seated because his statement is so damn on point. She's not going to be an easy catch for any man. Wild doesn't even begin to describe my sister, and that's probably what I love about her most.

"Not funny," Luna snaps as the table erupts in laughter at her expense.

"I have to go to the bathroom," I announce, pushing my chair back.

"I'll come," Luna says, but I put my hand on her shoulder and push her back down.

"I need a minute alone."

She puts her ass back in her chair, studying my face and seeing something that makes her say, "Okay."

I don't need to look Dylan's way to know he's watching me and every move I make. I can feel the heat from his gaze all the way across the room. Somehow, I keep my head high and eyes forward, concentrating on every step I take. I will not show any emotions. I won't let him know that I felt any pain when I woke up without him or his palpable silence afterward.

Once inside the bathroom and behind the closed door, I lean over the countertop, trying to catch my breath. Seeing him hurts more than I expected since I've only known him for a few short days.

Anger, hurt, longing, and a dozen other emotions crash over me all at once. I'm being irrational about someone who's almost a stranger, but the sting is there, lodged deep in my chest.

I lift my head, looking at myself in the mirror. I look cute tonight. My dirty-blond hair is pinned up in a bun that's made up of twisted braid. It's a crazy hairstyle I found on the internet, and somehow, I'm able to pull it off without looking like a complete weirdo. My makeup is flawless, and my eye shadow makes my blue eyes pop.

I am going to march out of here and make Dylan regret walking out and ghosting me the last few days without so much as an I'm sorry. Pulling my lip gloss from my purse, I give my lips a once-over to make them extra shiny and even more noticeable.

Eat your heart out, Dylan Walsh.

The shirt I have on shows a small amount of cleavage, but I give it a good yank, exposing more of my breasts before I walk out the door and into the long hallway. I'm halfway back to the bar when a hand grabs me around the waist, hauling me backward.

I yelp and somehow maintain my footing even though he's more powerful than I am. "Dylan, this isn't how you get me back."

I glance down and realize my mistake immediately. It's not Dylan's ink and not his arm around me either. "Shut up, bitch," he growls before clamping his hand over my mouth, making it impossible for anyone to hear me scream.

But I try anyway, clawing at his hand, hoping someone will hear me over the music and nonstop voices filling the bar. The few sips of beer I drank before I left the table climb up my throat, filling my mouth with nowhere to go. I swallow it down, my stomach instantly revolting, but I scream again, ignoring the pain.

The man's arm tightens around my stomach underneath my ribs, winding me. "If you don't stop, I'm going to knock your ass out. But that would be a pity because I wouldn't be able to see the fear in your eyes at what I have planned for you."

I kick my feet back, making it easier for him to carry me, and I don't land a single blow that does a damn. He opens a door, throwing me into the darkened room before he joins me, slamming the door behind us.

I climb to my feet, coming face-to-face with a man I know and will never forget. "You," I whisper, backing up even though there's no escape.

"You owe me, bitch." He licks his lips, looking at me in a way I never want to see another man look at me. His face is still messed up from Dylan's beating, but I will never forget what he looks like.

"Please don't do this," I beg, not wanting to go another round with this asshole. "Let me go, and I won't say anything to anyone."

He laughs, moving toward me and pinning me against a table. "Not until you pay up."

My chin trembles, and my breathing is fast, coming out through my nose and reeking of vomit. I lean back, almost flattening myself against the table to get away from his touch. "Name your price. I'll pay anything."

He pushes my legs apart, placing his body between them. "A rich bitch too."

My chest burns more with each passing second and every agonizing, panicked breath. "Whatever it is, I'll pay. Just let me go. Please," I plead with him.

His hand goes to my jeans, and he grabs the button. "I only want a piece of the sweet pussy everyone seems to be fighting over."

Oh my God. No. No. No.

I'm not weak. I know better than this. My father and uncles taught me how to protect myself, but that day at the Caves, he caught me off guard. That shit is not going to happen twice.

The fear leaves me, and anger takes over.

I reach up and dig my nails into the skin of his face, tearing at his flesh as I lift my knee, getting him right in the balls. "Fuck you," I hiss as he rolls over, falling to the floor in agony.

He howls, holding his junk, his face bleeding again, but this time, because of me. I don't stick around to rub it in his face that I was the one to take him down this time.

I run for the door, flinging it open, and smash into a tall, hard body.

"Wildcat," he whispers, and I glance up with wide eyes. "What the…" He looks beyond me and into the room. "Go to your family, and I'll take care of him."

I grab his shirt, needing the contact and to give him the assurance that I'm okay. "I didn't… He didn't…"

He brushes the hair away from my eyes. "Don't worry, Ro. Go to your family. I'll take care of him. Go."

I don't waste another moment before taking off down the hallway, not looking back, and head straight for the table. By the time I make it, I'm out of breath, panting, and sweating.

"What the fuck, Ro?" Luna asks, her gaze moving from my face to my hands. "Why do you have blood on your fingers?"

"Man…" I point toward the hallway. "He…"

Every guy at the table stands and runs toward the hallway without another word or all the information.

Based on the looks on everyone's faces, I'm pretty damn sure no other explanation is needed.

Gigi stands and wraps an arm around me, comforting me.

"He didn't…"

"Shh, baby. We got you," she says softly.

"I got away," I stammer as my body shakes, the reality of what happened and my escape finally crashing over me.

"Call Uncle James and Thomas," Gigi says, rubbing my back slowly. "We need them here."

"On it," Rebel says, picking up her phone and walking away from the table.

"I kicked him and got away before he could…" I can't say the word. He was going to rape me as payback for the other day.

"You're okay," Gigi keeps repeating. "You did good."

And I did.

I did what I was taught, remembering to go for the face and balls if any man bothered me. Those are the two weakest points, and I used them to my advantage.

"Dylan's back there," I whisper to my sister as I look up into her soft eyes. "He found me."

She rocks me back and forth for a moment until my body isn't shaking quite as bad. "We should go wait outside for Uncle James and Thomas."

I nod, sick of talking and still trying to slow down my heart, which has been pounding for what feels like hours instead of minutes. People in the bar are staring at us as Gigi helps me to the door, followed by every other woman from our table. The men are still busy doing whatever unholy things they want to the asshole who attacked me.

He deserves whatever he gets, too. I'm sure I'm not his first victim. He already has a track record, trying to drug Luna and then hitting me. Tonight is just another day in the life of a slimeball, but his extracurricular activities are about to come to an end.

Rocco's right behind us as we all make it outside. "He's secured in the storage room until James and Thomas get here."

"Why didn't we just call the cops?" Rebel asks. "I'm sure they could be of more help."

Nick shakes his head. "Uncle Joe's coming too."

My stomach drops again. "Oh God," I groan.

"Oh boy," Gigi says, holding me tighter. "This is going to turn into a real shitshow in a hot minute."

"Don't let them get in trouble," I beg my sister.

Gigi smiles down at me as we sit on the sidewalk like two drunkards. "Baby, Dad, Uncle James, and Uncle Thomas know what they're doing. Don't ask how I know, but have faith they'll do the right thing… whatever they feel is the right thing, at least."

Three cars come blazing into the parking lot like

they were all racing to get here first. Dad's the first one out, running to me with Uncle James and Thomas right behind him.

He kneels down, staring me straight in the eyes with such tenderness. "You okay, baby?"

"I'm fine, Daddy. I got away. I remembered what you taught me. Face and balls."

He touches my cheeks, giving me a small smile. "Good girl."

I smile back, some of the fear from earlier evaporating. "I listened."

"I know, honey. You always do. You going to be okay out here while I go inside?"

I nod. "Don't do anything…"

"Shh. You just worry about yourself. We'll do the rest," he tells me.

"That's what I'm afraid of," I mutter as he follows my two uncles into the bar. "This is bad. It's going to be bad."

All my female cousins are standing around guessing at what's happening inside, but they don't have to wait long because the rest of the men file out, minus my dad, James, and Thomas.

"What's happening?" I ask Pike.

He shakes his head and sits down next to Gigi. "None of my business. It's in their hands now."

The gravel near my feet moves as Dylan sits down next to me. "I'm going to take her home," he announces to everyone like it's that damn simple.

"Um. No, you're not," I reply immediately, staring at him like he's off his rocker.

His eyes search mine, but I can see the determination on his face. "Wildcat, we have shit to talk about, and I'm not waiting another minute to say what needs to be said."

"Go with Dylan, and I'll look after Dad," Gigi says, letting me go.

I turn to her with a glare. "Excuse me?"

She leans over so only I can hear her. "Come on, Ro. You like him. He's saved you twice now. Let him baby you and grovel all night for your forgiveness. After that, if you want to kick his ass to the curb, at least you're doing it on your terms," she whispers.

I stare at her, my lips twisting. "I don't know."

"Ro, please," he begs at my side.

Gigi winks. "And let the groveling commence. Don't go easy on him."

"I don't know if I'm in the mood to play hardball, sis."

"You do whatever you want," she tells me, bumping into me with her shoulder. "Just get some rest and try to relax. Make him rub your feet or some shit."

Dylan stands, holding out a hand to me. "Come on, baby."

I turn toward him, my face not soft or friendly. After staring at him for a few seconds, I slide my hand into his, letting him pull me up from the ground. "Don't you have to work?" I ask.

"Fuck no. I was only here as an extra hand as a favor. It's not like it's busy."

"Don't get any ideas about tonight. I'm still pissed at you," I remind him.

"I know," he says, but instead of letting me walk, he lifts me into his arms and starts walking toward his brother's truck. "I have a lot to make up for and even more explaining to do. Just give me tonight to do it."

I want to say something, but it feels too good being in his arms. For the first time, I finally relax, letting the safety of his size and warmth pull me under.

Dylan has me...

I am physically safe, but my heart is not.

DYLAN

WE'RE ALMOST BACK to Rosie's apartment, and we haven't spoken a word to each other since I started the engine. I'm so angry—at myself, at the man who attacked her for a second time, at the world.

Hell, I'm even pissed at my father for fucking up my head and my heart so badly, I do dumb shit like pushing away my chance at something freaking spectacular.

"What happened back there?" she asks me.

I glance over at Rosie as the lights from oncoming cars sweep across her tear-stained face. "Don't worry about it, wildcat. Between your family and me, he'll never lay hands on you again."

"I've heard that before," she mutters.

I tighten my fingers around the steering wheel as I remember the terror in her eyes when the door opened. "I have no doubt what I started, your uncles and father finished."

"You mean, what I started?"

The smallest smile spreads across my lips at her words. "What you started," I correct my statement. "We just came in to clean up afterward, something that should've been done the first time he laid hands on you."

Rosie places her elbow on the door, resting her cheek against her fingers with her gaze straight ahead. "I didn't even see him there before I went to the bathroom. It's as if he materialized out of nowhere like a nightmare, waiting for his moment to strike."

"I didn't see him either," I tell her, playing back the time I spent at the door until I saw Rosie walk in and coming up blank. He must've seen her or me first, deciding to lurk in the back, waiting on the perfect moment to strike.

"I thought he was you at first," she says.

Her words are like a punch to my fucking gut. "I'd never hurt you like that, Ro."

"He didn't hurt me right away. He caught me off guard, wrapping his arms around my waist. I didn't try to get away, thinking it was you behind me, trying to make amends. But I had been so pissed at you, I wasn't paying attention to who was around me, and well…you know what happened."

I smack the steering wheel with the meaty part of my palm, pissed at myself for being such an asshole.

She startles at my sudden movement, doubling my guilt.

"This is my fault," I tell her. "If I hadn't…"

She reaches across the cab of the truck, placing her fingers on my forearm. "What happened tonight isn't your fault, Dylan."

"If I hadn't pissed you off, you wouldn't have been there. Or if you were, I would've been by your side."

"If I weren't pissed at you and you were by my side, you wouldn't have gone to the bathroom with me. He still would've been waiting for me when I walked out of there alone," she explains rationally and calmly, two things I'm not in this moment. "You can't be with me every minute of every day."

"Did he…" I swallow the words, finding any possibility of her being hurt again painful, and look back at her.

She shakes her head. "At first, I froze and then begged. But then I remembered what my dad taught me and used the training he drilled into us at a young age. I may not have the strength to last long, but I knew how to cause him enough pain in a short burst to allow myself an escape."

"Fuck," I hiss, hating that it's something she had to be taught to do.

"We're always taught to be on guard…as women."

"That's some crazy bullshit," I grumble, gripping the steering wheel tighter to alleviate my anger.

She shrugs her shoulder closest to me. "Men have no clue what it's like constantly looking over your shoulder, waiting for someone to try something."

"I've never…"

"Of course you haven't. You're a man. It's not like a woman is going to attack you out of nowhere and try to spear themselves on your dick. You're the top of the food chain. You're the predator and not the prey. If you lived your life like the prey, you'd have a whole new experience."

"I had that life when I was a kid," I whisper, realizing my father was the predator in my life for the first eighteen years until I'd had enough. But I never had to wonder who was preying on me. I only had to wonder when he would pounce, which was more often than I care to remember and have tried to block out.

"It's the same for us, but for our entire lives. We can never grow out of it and can only learn how to defend ourselves from an attack. But instead of worrying only about being physically assaulted, we have to fear being raped too."

I've never hated being a man until this moment. I've never put much thought into how women feel or what they worry about in different situations. I've never walked around looking over my shoulder, wondering if the next person I passed would be the one to put hands on me.

Growing up, I always knew who my attacker was going to be. The only thing I could do was try to read his moods, learning when he was most likely to strike and preparing myself for the inevitable onslaught. It took me over a decade to nail down the warning signs, but it never made the beatings any easier to take.

"I'm sorry," I whisper, my head swimming with so many thoughts about my past and her everyday reality.

"For what?" she asks

"That you have to walk around always looking over your shoulder because of assholes like me."

"I don't live in a constant state of paranoia. It's more like awareness. I'm careful, checking my surroundings when I'm alone, especially at night. I'm not always afraid. There have only been a handful of times in my life when I was truly fearful, and the two times I've been attacked, I wasn't even the least bit suspicious or concerned. That's the fucking insane thing about it all. I wasn't paying attention. I let my guard down."

"Don't you dare blame yourself for what happened," I tell her, pulling into her apartment complex. "A predator will find a way, and there's nothing you can do to stop it."

"I know," she whispers, turning her face away from me and toward the passenger side window.

"All that matters is that you were able to give yourself the opportunity to get away, and hopefully you'll never be put in that spot again."

"Yeah," she says softly, her voice shaking a little on the single word.

We sit in silence, me lost in my anger and her lost in more emotions than I'll ever be able to understand, as I drive the last hundred feet to an open parking spot near her building.

When I cut the engine and climb out, Ro isn't quick to get out. She opens the door to the truck, but her ass stays in the seat as if she's unable or unwilling to move. I stalk around the front and round the truck, finding her staring at the ground as if it's about to swallow her whole.

"Ro?"

She lifts her face, tears streaming down her cheeks. "He could've really hurt me."

I reach out, placing my open palm against her face, and she leans into my touch. "I know, but he didn't."

"That could've ended so many other ways."

"I know, baby, but it didn't."

"What if you hadn't…"

"You still would've gotten away. I wasn't the one who clawed at his face and kneed him in his junk."

Her gaze sweeps across my face, her eyes searching mine for something.

"You did that, Ro. You hurt him, hard and deep enough to get away from him. That wasn't me, baby —that was you," I remind her, wanting her to feel empowerment, if that is even possible, about what happened instead of victimized.

She blinks, the tears still running wild and free. "I did do that, didn't I?" Her voice is soft and distant, as if she's replaying every awful moment that happened tonight.

I drop my hand from her face, moving my arms to her back and legs. "You did," I tell her as I scoop her into my arms.

She doesn't fight me when I lift her out of the truck. One of her arms loops around my neck as if we've done this a million times before and are working on muscle memory and instinct. She places her head against my chest, melting into me as if I am her sanctuary and safety, neither sentiment I've earned yet.

I kick the truck door closed with my boot before marching toward her apartment, knowing I want a relationship like this but at a time when there's not a crisis or a threat to her very existence.

She goes silent as I carry her toward her front

door, reaching into her purse to retrieve the key when we're a few feet away.

"I'm going to take care of you, Rosie," I promise her, knowing I'm not going to leave her side again.

"Like you did last time?" she asks as I balance her in my arms and unlock the door at the same time.

The blow may have been low, but it is totally deserved. I did an asshole thing, taking off after we had sex, and I'm not even sure my reasoning could be understood by anyone except me. I'll try, though. It's all I can do. Explain everything to her and pray she forgives me, allowing me to take part in her life even if it's only in a small way.

I don't reply right away, stewing in my feelings and giving myself a verbal ass-whooping as I carry her inside. I walk straight to her bedroom, her still in my arms, and sit down on the bed, but I don't let go of her. "Not like last time, wildcat."

She peers up, her big blue eyes swimming with emotion. "You sure about that? Now's your chance to run."

I shake my head, tightening my grip on her body and cradling her more. "What I did was wrong. There was no reason for me to run away like a scared-ass pussy."

She sits up a little, drying her cheeks with the backs of her fingers. "It was shitty, Dylan."

Good. She is no longer sad. I'd rather her be

pissed at me than sad or scared like she was earlier. As long as she's focused on me, she can't fret over what almost happened in the bar.

"I know, baby. I know."

"Why would you do that?"

I keep one hand around her bottom, resting my hand on her thigh, and place my other one around her front so they cross. "Because I was an idiot."

"Well, obviously," she mutters. "But I thought what happened the night before was amazing, and then you vanished without a word."

"I was scared," I confess, hating to admit to that feeling to anyone ever.

"Of liking me?"

I shake my head. "I'll admit that every day of the week, Rosie. I more than like you, but I was scared of what I saw in the morning when I rolled over."

Her eyebrows pull down in the middle, and I replay my last statement, immediately realizing my mistake.

"No, wildcat. Not *who* I saw, but *what* I saw. The night before was—" I pause, my dick hardening at the memories of fucking her against the wall "—fucking amazing. Mind-blowing, even. But when I saw the bruises running up and down your back, knowing I put them there... I freaked out and ran. I couldn't stop myself after I knew I hurt you."

She lifts her hand to my face, so sweet and tender. "You didn't hurt me, Dylan."

I lean forward, placing my forehead against hers. "I spent my childhood covered in bruises, and I promised myself I'd never be *that* guy. When I saw what I'd done, all I could think about was my dad and how I could become him, or maybe that I was becoming him, and I panicked."

She slowly glides her fingers through my beard as I confess what I felt and feared. "You aren't him."

"But what if I'll become him? What if I *am* becoming him?"

She pulls away, staring into my eyes. "Have you ever hurt someone on purpose who didn't deserve it?"

"I'm sure if you could raise my old man from the dead and ask him, he'd probably say I deserved every beating I got, Ro."

Her frown is immediate, but her eyes never leave me, and neither does her touch. "He was an asshole. You are nothing like him. You are kind, caring, and thoughtful. You're a protector, not an abuser."

"But your bruises…"

"Were a reminder of the best sex I've ever had. They don't even hurt much, Dylan. I forget they're there. And then I'll move a certain way, and all I can think about is the way you fucked me, the look in your eyes when you did it, and the pleasure you gave me…

repeatedly." She smiles, and my chest aches at the sweetness of her words and purity in her heart.

She's a good person from an amazing family raised by great parents. I don't deserve something so perfectly beautiful in my life, but I'm not willing or able to let her go.

"I realized—too late, I might add—that I shouldn't have run away from you. I know I'm not my father, but sometimes I allow that fear to creep in that I could be. I never want to be the person who makes you cry, but I realized I already did that when I left you. I didn't consider your feelings or what you wanted. I only cared about myself and what I felt. As soon as I realized I fucked up, I knew I had to apologize and beg for your forgiveness. There's nothing more I want in my life except you and a chance to be worthy of your love. I'm begging you to give me another chance to prove I deserve having you in my life."

"Dylan," she whispers, and the sound of my name guts me.

She's going to turn me down.

I've fucked up way too much. The cut is too deep to climb out of, no matter how much I apologize or what I do. Some wounds are too big to overcome with a simple apology.

She leans into me, her hand on my face, caressing my skin. "I want this. I want us. You don't need to beg. I just want honesty, and you're giving that to me. But I need you to hear me and understand—you did not hurt me the other night, no matter what you saw on my back. You need to trust me to tell you if I'm ever worried or in fear, and I'll trust you to tell me when you're scared or panicked. You need to stop running and settle in and allow yourself to be happy."

I cup her face in my hands, breathing hard and fast. "You'll give me another chance?"

"I don't know if I've even had time to give up on you. I hoped you'd come to your senses eventually, but I was pissed that you didn't talk to me and I was worried you wouldn't open up. But yes, I'll give you another chance. I feel safe with you. Safer than anyone else has ever made me feel."

"I promise to be worthy of that feeling, Ro. All I know is whatever is happening between us, it's too powerful to throw away. It's too strong to ignore. The pull to you is something I've never felt with anyone else."

"There's something magical here," she whispers.

"Is that what this is?" I ask.

She nods. "I think so. I don't know any other way to describe it."

The moment is too heavy, an emotion I've never done well. "So, I'm the best you've ever had?"

"You're such an asshole."

"We've been over that and agree. But seriously, the best ever?"

She smacks me playfully. "I don't know. Let's try again and see if it was a fluke. I mean, maybe you're awful at—"

I move quickly, covering her mouth with mine. "Lies," I murmur against her lips. "I'm the best you've ever had and will ever have, baby. You're mine now, and I'm going to make sure you're ruined for any other man."

"Challenge accepted," she murmurs back, and we fall into a kiss, long and deep, as if the last few horrible hours never happened.

ROSIE

"Wait," he says. "Not so fast."

His hand is on mine, tugging my fingers away from his belt. Slowing me down from what I want.

"What's wrong?" I ask. I don't move my hands away, but I let the strength of his grip hold me tight against him.

Now that this thing is real, now that we've put words to the mess of feelings behind us, I want to consume him. What is he waiting for? Is he doubting what we've shared?

His eyes flash, and he tightens his fists over my fingers. "We're gonna take our time. This is different, you and me. Not like before."

Before… Fuck, it was hot, raw, and rough. So rough. I clench my pussy just remembering the feeling of my back against the wall, his weight pinning me in place, his cock so deep that nothing except the sweat, the pressure, and the heat made sense.

A surge of arousal floods my core as I remember that night. But now...he wants *different*. Maybe he wants more.

"Okay." I agree, and he releases me, but only so he can pull me into his arms and hold me.

"Never forget this." He grits out the words as he presses his forehead to mine. "What this feels like. I want you chasing this high for the rest of our lives."

"As if I could ever forget." I whisper the words, but I know he hears them.

He closes his eyes and fists his hands in my hair, one hand on either side of my head. He moves my head so my chin lifts and my eyes close. I suck my lower lip into my mouth and wet it, biting down lightly to focus my brain on a single point of pressure, a single point of almost pain that will slow down the racing beat of my heart in my chest.

"If you do," he grunts, "I'll remind you. Always."

With every heavy whisper, the heat of his breath feathers my skin. The scent of him, fresh air, clean bedsheets, and the smoky smell of his skin weaken my resolve to let him show me how he wants me.

To be patient is my torture, but I am. I must be.

I keep my eyes closed, my hair still firmly between his reverent fingers. I don't need to open my eyes to know he's closing in on my mouth. The electric heat between us sparks in the agonizing seconds before he takes me and claims me as his.

His first kiss is a tease against my lips. I lift my chin to taste more of him. I'm that starving woman at the banquet, my mouth open and hungry to taste it all, but he feeds me nibbles, little tastes. My lower lip between his teeth. The flick of his tongue to open me.

I have to be patient, to sample his lips, soft as they explore mine.

"Baby," he groans. "I want to savor this. Take my time. When you make that sound…"

I hadn't even realized I was humming, a half-begging moan as I kissed him back. I giggle. "It seems only fair. I was ready to tear your pants off a minute ago, but you stopped me."

"Too much talking," he says, bending his mouth to my neck. "I wanna hear that sound again." He flicks his tongue along the curve of my neck. "Fuck, yes," he hisses. "That's the way, wildcat."

I lose myself in the scorching power his lips have over my body. I grab the back of his head and press my hips against his, arching my neck back to give him access to more of me. I extend myself like an invitation—he can have it all. I'm his, body and soul. Heart and mind. His lips mark my neck, and then I feel his teeth, his tongue, nibbling and teasing my skin until my skin pebbles and my knees tremble.

I can feel his cock through his jeans, straining

against the denim, pressing against the front of my blouse. I take the throb of his erection against me as an invitation and reach a hand between us, ready to palm him through his pants, but he stops me again.

"You first," he insists. "But I want to watch."

"Watch me what?" I ask.

He stands and steps away from me, and it's as if someone has thrown a blanket over the sun. A different kind of chill invades my body, but he doesn't break our contact for long.

He puts two fingers under my chin and lifts my face so our eyes meet. "Take off your shirt," he says. He crosses his arms over his massive chest and waits.

I whip the damn scrap of fabric over my head and toss it aside. His face is pure lust. My bra is sheer; my nipples pebbled hard; the dusky outlines easily visible through the barely-there lace.

"Fuck," he groans. "Change of plans."

He bends and sweeps me into his arms, then sets me gently on my bed. He unfastens his belt and drops his jeans. He's not wearing underwear, and his cock greets me happily, the bob of his impressive length reminding me of the last time. My body responds to the memory, to the sight, and to the anticipation.

He's mine.

He'll be mine forever.

I can't look away, transfixed by his beauty, his power.

His muscular torso twists as he yanks off his T-shirt.

"Baaaaaby," I mewl, begging him like the greedy bitch I am. I rub my thighs together as I watch him from bed.

I'm so wet just watching him, I can't take it. My jeans are still on, but with the air on my bra, what little there is of it, I'm aching everywhere. My back arches, I'm curling my toes... Fuck, I might come if he just breathes on me at this rate.

But it's good. It's so good, the way he climbs onto my bed, kneels above me, straddling my body with his legs. His cock is so close, it nearly grazes my chest, and I try to wiggle my ass on the mattress to bring that tasty tip to my mouth. The barbell that's pierced through the tiny ridge of tender skin on the underside of the head beckons to my lips. I want to tug that silver stud between my teeth, licking to soothe against the sensation until he cries my name, but again, he stops me.

"I wanna ravish your tits until you scream," he promises. "And then, I'm gonna taste your come. After that, you can do what you want."

"Too much talking," I grit out, but I smile as I echo what he said to me earlier.

He holds both my wrists above my head against the mattress and adjusts his weight so his mouth is over my lacy cups. He tears away the fabric with his teeth and masterfully flicks the tip of one nipple with his tongue. I lose my breath and thrash against the hold he has on me, but it's all instinct, all reaction.

I love it. I love him.

I love the flood of pleasure that pours from his mouth, nipping and laving my exposed tip raw. No one else could make my body react this way.

This is him. This is me. Us.

The lava in my core, the breathlessness of every second I wait for him to suck me deeper into his sweet, hot mouth, is so pure, I squint against real tears.

"Baby," I beg. "Oh God, baby."

He knows just when to switch to my right breast, the cool air meeting my swollen nipple and bringing with it another kind of sensual agony.

He releases my hands so he can cup both breasts, squeezing and sucking, kneading, and nipping until I've got my legs around his hips and am grinding against his length.

My jeans are a horrible barrier, my drenched panties sticky with the evidence of my want.

We're wordlessly in tune as he tugs his mouth away from my tits and unbuttons my jeans, one agonizing button at a time. His face is flushed now, his lips puffy from working my body, and I want that mouth, those perfect, sensual lips, to taste the effect he has on me.

I don't have to tell him, because he's already between my legs. My panties are on as he strokes his fingers along the insides of my thighs.

"Fuck," he hisses. "I could come just smelling you."

I reach for my underwear, wishing he'd shred my panties the way he did my bra, but he swats my hand away.

"Mine," he growls.

As if he's read my mind, my panties are gone, literally, two scraps of fabric that split open at the seams under his fists. I know the feeling because right now, I want to burst, explode against the confinement of this pent-up need.

He tosses my panties, or what's left of them, on the floor and kneels between my legs on the bed. His gaze is burning hot, and he puts one palm on the inside of each thigh and spreads my legs wide. He watches, taking in my trimmed pussy, the wetness of my arousal nearly dripping onto the bed. My legs quiver under his hot hands, but he holds them there and just looks.

His raw appraisal makes me feel even hotter, and I open my legs wider, tempting him to take all that's his. And oh, does he take me. He drops his face to my pussy and breathes against the tender skin.

The cool air blasts my nerve endings before his tongue strokes liquid fire along my seam.

I buck against his palms, but he's holding me firm, keeping me open. Now he's the lion, and I am the meal as he feasts on my body. He flicks my clit with his tongue, lapping me until I'm even wetter.

I'm so on fire with need, I'm trembling and begging. Sounds are spilling from my mouth, my thighs are fighting a war they can't win, but I'm no longer in control of my reactions. My body shakes and moans and moves as he wants it to, responding to him and him alone. When he frees one thigh, it's only to move his hand to pinch my swollen clit between two fingers.

"Holy fuck!" I nearly launch off the bed, but I quickly settle back into a rhythm. His mouth against my opening, his fingers on my clit, and then, before I can prepare myself, three fingers thrust knuckle-deep inside. He doesn't go in easy but hard, tugging his fingers against my walls until I'm shuddering and screaming, pulling his hair as I ride his face.

But I don't just come once. He's not going to let that happen. As soon as I stop screaming, he's kneeling over me, his cock dangling against my mouth.

"Open," he commands.

As if he even has to ask.

I lick my lips and grip his shaft with one hand. While I stroke the underside of his balls with the other hand, I lap my tongue against the tender pierced foreskin. I take the length of him into my mouth and wet him. When I close my lips around him, the piercing creates the slightest resistance, and he sucks in air, cursing and holding on to the wall behind the bed for support.

"Enough," he grunts.

He's on his back and tugs me up to sitting.

"Get on," he demands. "I wanna watch your perfect fucking body while you ride me."

I want the exact same thing. But not yet. I kneel above his chest, my tits raw from his teeth and tongue, my pussy already sated but somehow still ready for more, for him. I hold his face in my hands and gently kiss his lips, his nose, his chin.

He lies there, letting me show him how much I love him, exploring all the different ways this new thing between us feels and sounds. His eyes are closed, but they fly open when I move away from his face.

He watches my every move as I straddle his hips. I lower myself onto him slowly, letting every inch of my body expand to fit his size. "Oh...fuck," I groan, dropping my head to his chest.

My hair falls into my face, and I'm dizzy as he fills me, his cock so long and thick, I can't believe I have to ride him. But as soon as I adjust, I'm ready. I clench my thighs and throw back my head. My sweaty hair tangles over my shoulders as I lace my fingers through his. He locks his elbows so I can use his strength, gripping his hands while I work my hips in lazy, sensual circles on his erection.

I grind and work my hips on his, and his face goes hazy, his eyes smoky with emotion, passion. I speed up, his length hitting just the right spot while I tip my hips forward so the pressure on my clit matches the perfection happening inside.

"Baby, fuck!" I come again and again, pleasure spreading through my body. My nipples feel alive, on fire, my thighs burn as I clench against him. When I finish, panting and sweating, I don't move, instead letting him take that moment to arch beneath me. He jerks his hips and thrusts, his sheer strength and size moving my body up and down on his cock. Our fingers still laced, my body flushed and raw, he roars, his essence flooding me. I feel the delicious drag of his stud inside me, adding that extra little bit of sensation that, fuck, we don't even need. It's dangerous how explosive we are together, and as we come down, cooling and sighing, it occurs to me that this is exactly what I thought I could have with him.

More than just fucking. More than just his enormous, tattooed body bringing mine the escape of a rough release. As I collapse against his chest, my knees are shaking and my thighs feel like twin rubber bands, loose and bendy.

He pulls me close, the smell of our sex heavy in the air. It's delicious and decadent. It's more than just his smoky-whiskey scent, the fresh air, clean sheets, and promises that made me want him in the first place. This is us, the union of what we become when we're one. As I wrap my arms around his sculpted chest, I let my eyes flutter shut.

This is it. I know it is.

This is us.

This is love.

And it's just the beginning.

22

DYLAN

I STOP WALKING, standing outside the front door with my fingers laced with Rosie's. "I don't know if this is a good idea."

She tugs me forward, twisting the knob. "Don't be silly. Everyone's expecting you, and they're excited."

"Everyone?" I ask, raising an eyebrow.

"Uh, yeah. The entire family is here."

I yank her backward as she starts to take a step.

She lets out an exaggerated grunt. "Seriously?"

I tilt my head, needing the affirmation so I don't walk into a shitshow without being prepared for the worst. "Even your dad? He's excited?"

She nods, leaning into me and running her free hand over my chest. "Even my dad."

I blink, still confused as fuck. The man has hated

me since the day he laid eyes on me. "You're lying to me, wildcat."

"He knows he's been wrong about you your entire life. We had a long talk, and he knows it's time to make amends."

"Make amends?" I repeat, no more clued-in than when we pulled in.

"He fucked up, and now he's going to make sure you know he's sorry."

My eyebrows rise. "He's going to apologize to me?"

She nods. "But I hope you're willing to do the same since you've called him an asshole more than once."

"Well, it's not like he was nice to me."

"He's not nice to anyone, Dylan." She flattens her palm on my chest, right over my heart. "You can either forgive each other and start fresh, or we're going to have a very long and tension-filled life. I'm a daddy's girl, and I always will be. So please, do me a favor and play nice."

I wrap my arm around her back with her hand still clasped in mine. The position makes her back arch, pushing her tits against me. "I can do nice, wildcat."

She laughs and smacks my front with her free hand. "I'm being serious."

I waggle my eyebrows. "So am I."

"Sweet Jesus. This is going to be a long day."

I lean forward, bending my neck, and place a soft, chaste kiss against her lips. "Nah. I'll be on my best behavior."

Her eyes flutter open, and she smiles up at me with the purest, most beautiful smile. When she looks at me, I forget all the bad shit in my past and think only about her and the good things in my life.

"Can we go in now? My makeup is starting to melt."

"You don't need to wear that shit on your face. You're so goddamn beautiful without it."

She rolls her eyes. "I wear it for me and you. I like it. Why? Do you hate it?"

I shake my head. "No, wildcat. I don't hate it, but I never want you to change who you are for me. I don't think there's a time when you're more stunning than when you first wake up in the morning."

"You're so full of shit," she mutters, finally pulling me into the foyer of her grandparents' house. "We're here!"

"Fuckin' great," I mutter, earning myself the stink eye from the princess of light.

"Behave."

"I didn't do anything," I say, toeing off my boots in the foyer and pushing them into the neat little row that takes up half the space.

How many freaking people are here? Based on the

number of shoes, sandals, and boots, it looks like half the town has taken up camp at the Gallo compound.

"Back here!" a woman yells back, but it isn't her grandmother's voice.

"Is your *entire* family here?" I ask, not moving as quickly as she'd like since she's pulling me forward with all her might.

"Yep. All of them."

"Fuck," I hiss, hating this.

Maybe if I'd grown up in a family instead of with only my father and brothers, I wouldn't be shit at being around other people's families. But here I am, shitty with my people skills and never one to worry about hurting any feelings. But I can do this. I did it the other night with her grandparents, and I didn't come off like a complete jackass.

"Dylan," her grandmother says, walking toward us with her arms extended.

I freeze for a second, because no one in my family greets one another with a hug. You're lucky if you get a damn hello or so much as a grunt of recognition.

"Hey," I say as my arms open on their own like she's somehow controlling my movements.

Her hug is firm and short before she backs away, still holding on to my arms. "We're so happy you're back."

"I'm honored to be here," I tell her, and I'm being sincere.

Rosie rolls her eyes again before laughing at me, knowing I'm on my best behavior and not acting entirely like myself.

"I hope you brought your appetite because if you leave here hungry, it's your own damn fault, baby."

I smile at her, loving the ease of the woman. "I'll eat everything I can."

"Good," she whispers.

"Lemme see him," a woman as old as Rosie's grandmother says, moving right past my girl without as much as a hello.

"Aunt Fran. Wait," Rosie says, holding up a hand. "Oh, forget it. Good luck," she says to me and laughs as she finally drops her arms.

I stare down as this little woman stalks right up to me, reaches out, and starts rubbing on me like we've known each other our entire lives and have been intimate for just as long too.

"Oh, he's nice," she says as her hands continue to roam. "Firm and young. Best combination."

"Dylan, this is our very handsy aunt Fran, Sal's sister," Grandma Gallo explains. "Don't pay her any attention. She just enjoys men and likes to piss off her husband."

My eyebrows go up immediately. "Her husband?" I ask, horrified as I glance around, waiting to get my ass kicked by an old man.

"You're from around here. Do you remember a

biker named Bear? He was probably already old before you left."

"Bear?" I whisper and swallow, feeling all the color drain from my face. "Um, yeah. He's kind of hard to forget."

"Woman," barks the voice I heard a dozen times as a kid, calling me a pissant and a nuisance. He stalks into the foyer with his eyes staring straight at Fran. "Can't you ever leave the young ones alone?"

"You mad?" she asks him and doesn't stop touching me. She doesn't even look his way to ask the question.

Fuuuck.

"Baby, I see I need to teach you another lesson about who you belong to."

She looks up at me with the sweetest smile and licks her lips. "You know how much I love that, baby. Sometimes I need a special reminder." She winks at me, and I almost die of embarrassment. "See," Fran whispers, giving me a wink. "Works every time."

"Walsh," Bear says, staring at me up and down as he wraps an arm around his woman and pulls her against him. "You haven't changed a bit in the last... what? Ten years?" He extends a hand to me, something he never did when I was young.

I stare down at his open palm, wondering and thinking it may be a trap. But then I give in, knowing

I have to trust someone eventually. "More like seven-teen, sir."

"Hmm. Manners? Never had them before," he says to me, raising one eyebrow as if he's not convinced I'm a different man than I was when I was eighteen.

"Growing up will do that to a person," I reply as he releases my hand, and Rosie slides up next to me, holding my arm.

"Be nice, Uncle Bear. I'm sure you're not like your eighteen-year-old self."

Bear laughs loudly. "I don't know how I survived. I had a death wish and a bad attitude."

Rosie's father enters the foyer with his wife next to him. "Attitude's still intact, old man," Joe says to Bear.

"Piss off with old-man shit." Bear ticks his chin toward Joe, eyeing the salt-and-pepper in his hair. "You aren't young anymore."

I'm so focused on Bear and Joe, I don't notice Suzy Gallo, Rosie's mom, as she walks up to us. And without warning, she pulls me into an embrace. "Thank you," she mutters into my T-shirt. "Thank you for saving our Rosie."

I peer over at Rosie, and she shrugs. "Go with it," she whispers. "She's emotional."

Suzy pulls her head back, glaring at her daughter. "And you're not? You cry every time the ASPCA commercial comes on television."

"Mom, those poor animals," Rosie says in the saddest voice. "I want to save them all."

"Oh, for fuck's sake. You two are every sob story's dream and total suckers. I don't even want to know how much you've sent them over the years," Joe says, running his hand down the side of his beard.

Suzy looks away from her husband and stares up at me with the same blue eyes as her daughter. "I hope you're hungry. We have a lot of food," she says, skating over the money issue for the animal charity.

"Famished, ma'am."

"Good." She smiles, deepening a few fine lines near her eyes.

"Dylan," Joe says, waiting for me to look his way, and when I do, he continues. "Can I talk to you a minute?"

Rosie squeezes my arm before releasing me, giving me my answer before I have a chance to reply. "Sure," I say, praying this doesn't end in disaster.

We've never had a civil conversation in my life, but I was also an asshole teenager, and he was an old man who complained about everything.

"We'll only be a minute, darling," Joe says to Rosie and not me. "I won't keep him. I promise."

Rosie nods before popping up on her tiptoes and kissing my cheek. "He's not a complete asshole," she whispers, reminding me. "I'll be waiting in the kitchen when you're done."

"Got it, wildcat," I tell her before looking to Joe.

He's standing near what seems to be a study off the foyer. "After you," he says with his arm extended.

I walk in, looking around at the rows upon rows of books and four leather chairs in a circle with a large wooden table in the middle.

"Sit," he tells me.

Never in a million years would I have believed I'd be seeing Rosie Gallo or that Joe Gallo wouldn't be acting like an absolute tool to me and warning his daughter away from me.

He did in the beginning. I heard the shitty things he said, but I no longer see the same distaste for me that he didn't bother to hide before.

He takes a seat opposite me and runs his hands up and down his thighs before leaning forward and staring straight at me. "First, I want to talk about the guy from the other night."

"Twice, he's laid hands on her, and twice, I've beaten him. He shouldn't—"

"He's been relocated," he says calmly.

I tilt my head and furrow my brows. "Relocated?"

He nods. "You'll never see him again."

I blink, staring at his calm demeanor, knowing those words don't mean the guy moved out of the town or state. "You…"

"I, nothing. The man won't be a problem again,

but I want to thank you for looking out for my daughter both times he touched her."

"She did most of the work the last time."

Joe smiles a proud papa smile, something I'd never been given from my own father. "She always was a quick learner and tougher than her twin."

"She's one of the best," I reply.

"I know I was an asshole to you in the past," he says, leaving any talk of the guy behind us.

Well, alrighty then.

I guess it's not my place to ask for more details. Secrets only stay secrets when as few people as possible know the information, and I'm clearly not part of the inner circle…yet.

"No, sir. You weren't."

He tilts his head the opposite direction as he leans back in the chair, staring at me with a look that says he knows I'm lying through my teeth. "I was wrong. I judged you based on the type of man your father was, and that wasn't right of me to do. You are not him, and you were a kid."

I stare back at him, unsure of what to say. "Well…"

He holds up a hand. "I know you hated me, which was fair. I was never kind to you when you were an older kid. When you were younger, I was, but then you turned into an angry, mouthy teenager."

"You would, too, if you grew up in my house."

He nods and drops his hand back to his leg. "I'm sure I would've been mouthier and angrier."

"Impossible," I mumble.

"When you were younger, I called Child Services a few times about what was happening at your house."

My eyes widen, never having known who made the calls. "It was you?"

"Yeah, kid. Saw shit that didn't sit right with me, but every time they came out, they didn't do shit. Figured maybe I was reading everything wrong."

I shake my head. "You weren't, but my old man was good at covering his tracks, and his drinking buddy had connections, making it damn near impossible for anyone to take us."

"I'm sorry about that."

I shrug. "Shit happens. What's in the past is staying there, buried with my old man. I appreciate you looking out for us, even though nothing came of it. Sure as hell pissed him off for a long time afterward. He always figured it was one of us who called. Took some beatings for it too."

A shadow passes across his face. "Fuck," he hisses, closing his eyes and taking a depth breath. When his eyes open again, the emotion is hidden. "I never meant for that to happen."

"In the past," I remind him. "Leave it there."

He nods, hopefully understanding what I'm

husband like she fully expected one of us to come out of the room bloodied.

"Sugar," he whispers, stalking over to her and sliding an arm around her waist. "You miss me?"

Suzy leans into him, something I'd often seen her do as a kid when they were in the yard. "I was worried."

"Don't worry, baby. I've mellowed with age."

"Thank God," she whispers, peering up at him in relief.

"You good?" Rosie asks me as I wrap my arms around her, pulling her into me.

"Couldn't be better."

She studies my face and must see something she likes and believes. "Good. Now, let's go. Everyone's waiting."

I place my fingers under her chin, forcing her to keep her eyes on me as I lean in and give her a soft and short kiss. "Thank you," I whisper.

"For what?" she asks, her blue eyes sparkling in the sunlight streaming through the foyer windows.

"For all of this and for being with me. For making me feel welcome and worthy. For giving me time with your family and not making me feel like an outsider."

"We'll see if you still feel that way after a little more time with my aunt Fran," she says, giggling.

"As long as Bear doesn't kick my ass, Fran can touch me all she wants, wildcat."

Rosie raises an eyebrow. "Be careful what you wish for, buddy."

"I love you, Rosie," I say softly so only she can hear. Words I've never spoken to another human in my entire life. Not my father and not even my brothers because we never said mushy shit around our house. No one in my entire life has made me feel welcome or even worth a damn, but Rosie Gallo does it.

I don't care that we've only spent a few days with each other. None of that matters. She makes me feel like I'm worthy of happiness, and saying those three words to her gives me more joy than anything I've ever said to anyone before.

"I love you too," she says easily and without hesitating before planting her lips on mine.

And for the first time in my entire life, I'm looking forward to the future and seeing a world of possibilities.

EPILOGUE

ROSIE

Almost One Year Later

Dylan leans over, staring at the small human in my arms, as he sits on the side of the hospital bed. "He's just so...so..."

"Perfect," I whisper, trying not to wake the baby. I'm exhausted after being in labor for twelve hours, but never happier than I am in this very moment.

"I was going to say tiny, but we can go with your words too," he says, smiling. "I mean, his face is smushed and his head is a little lopsided, but if you say he's perfect, then he is."

I stare up at my husband, loving and hating his brutal honesty. "Dylan," I warn, not having my usual sense of humor because I feel as if my body's been through a war.

He lifts his hand, moving the blanket away from our baby boy's face. "He's beautiful like his momma."

"I don't feel beautiful," I mutter, knowing I look like shit because I feel like it too.

Dylan peers up, staring at me the same way he did the first time he told me he loved me. "I've never seen a creature more beautiful than you are now. You did something I can never do. You gave me a gift which I can never give to you."

"Baby, he wouldn't be in my arms if it weren't for you. I didn't make him alone."

"I didn't grow him inside me, Ro. I didn't keep him safe and healthy for the last nine months."

"You kept us safe and healthy," I tell him, holding out the baby to Dylan. "Take him."

Dylan slides his arm underneath our son with ease, having had practice with his younger brothers when he was just a kid himself. "I take it back," he says to me as I yawn. "He's perfect."

I smile, my eyes getting heavy, but I force them to stay open. "He's like his daddy."

"Nah, Momma. This one's all you."

I relax into the bed, watching my two men together for the first time. "Does he look like a Salvatore?"

There's a softness on Dylan's face I usually only see when he's looking at me. "It fits him perfectly.

Your grandfather may have more hair, but I hope our little boy has the same wisdom and heart as the old guy."

"You better not let him hear you call him old."

"He's like a hundred years old, Ro. I think he knows."

I chuckle and don't even have the energy to smack him. "He's not that old."

Dylan gets up from the bed, holding our little man in his arms. He sways slowly, rocking our little boy gently in his arms. "Welcome to the world, Salvatore Joseph," he says softly, looking at Sal like he's the most precious and important thing he's ever laid eyes on. "I promise to always love and protect you, giving you all the love you deserve and more. You couldn't have a better mommy."

"Or daddy," I add, watching my two men.

"I hope I'm worthy of him, Ro," Dylan replies, running his fingers over the smattering of strawberry-blond hair on top of Sal's head. "I had a shit role model."

"You're not him, Dylan."

He peers over at me, staying in constant motion. "I know, love. I know. And if this would've happened a year ago, I would've been freaking the fuck out, but being part of your family changed me."

"You were always that man underneath."

Dylan stops and slides back into the bed with me. "You brought him out, reminding me of who I was. Without you…"

I place my hand on his arm, soaking in the sweet face of our boy. "We never have to worry about what could've been. This is how it is supposed to be."

Dylan shakes his head, smiling from ear to ear. "Salvatore Joseph Gallo," he whispers in awe.

"There's something so beautiful about that name."

"You know your family thinks we're a little off in the head," he tells me. "Men don't usually take their wife's last name."

I nod. "I wouldn't have it any other way."

When we went to fill out our marriage license a few days after we found out we were expecting, Dylan made it clear to the county clerk that I wouldn't be taking his name. He felt Walsh was tainted, and he didn't want the stigma in town to follow our kid into his future. He insisted that he take my name, passing it down to our children instead, and to say I was beside myself with joy is an understatement.

"You made Dad happy," I say.

He smiles. "The old guy is a sap for sure."

"You got major brownie points for that stunt, and I'm pretty sure you can never do any wrong in his eyes anymore."

"Oh, I'm sure I'll fuck up at some point."

"Hello," Luna says, knocking on the hospital room door as she pops her head inside.

Her hair is a mess, wild and matted on one side, and her lipstick is smeared. "Can we come in?"

"We?" I ask.

She laughs, opening the door for Ian to stick his head inside the room too.

"Nice shade," Dylan tells his brother as we see where Luna's lipstick has gone.

"Oh Jesus," I mumble. "You're going to give Dad a heart attack."

Ian lifts his black T-shirt, wiping away what Luna calls the perfect shade of red from his lips. "We were just passing time. We've been here for hours."

"You know," I say, staring at them with nothing but love, "most people would talk to fill the hours."

"Not that much to say," Luna informs me as she walks softly into the room like she's scared of waking a sleeping giant. "And sex is way more fun too."

"Can't argue that," Ian agrees with her. "I don't like spending too much time in this place after…" Ian shivers, having spent way too many days and nights inside these walls, battling and eventually overcoming his cancer, thanks to Dylan's bone marrow.

"I wanted to take his mind off being here," Luna adds, pulling a small mirror from her purse and fixing her face.

"Mission accomplished," Ian says, winking at her. "Memories have been changed."

"You two a couple now?" I ask.

They both shake their heads.

"Just fuck buddies?" Dylan asks.

"It was a one-time thing," Luna says as she walks up to Dylan and Sal and stares down at her new nephew. "He's beautiful."

"Where're Mom and Dad?" I ask, surprised the room isn't full of people by now.

"They nodded off in the waiting room, and I didn't have the heart to wake them. Plus, I was being selfish, wanting a few minutes with my twin before our lives change forever and the insanity starts."

I lift my arm, motioning for her to come sit with me. "Some things will never change, Lu."

She leans into me, placing her head against my shoulder. "You're a mom now, Ro."

"You will be someday too."

"Fuck you," she whispers. "Don't curse me like that."

"You have to settle down sometime," I remind her because the years keep ticking by faster and faster.

"I do not. There's so little time and so many men." She peers up at me with a devilish smile. "I'm not done wreaking havoc on the opposite sex, babe."

"And when you are finished?"

"I don't know if that's possible."

We laugh like old times. "Lord help the man who finally catches you."

"He better be a strong one because I'm not going to make it easy," she says softly.

"I wouldn't expect anything less."

"But when I finally find him," she says, looking toward Dylan and Ian, "I hope he loves me half as much as that man loves you, sissy."

"He'll love you, and you'll love him more than you ever thought possible."

"I won't go easy."

The obstetrician walks in, and the air inside the room shifts as he locks eyes with Luna. "Ms. Gallo," he says, holding my chart in one hand as he stops walking.

"Yes," Luna and I say in unison.

He blinks, gawking at my sister, and I recognize the look in his eyes. He's smitten. Something Luna is able to do to most men.

She sits up, brushing her hair away from her shoulder, all needy for a man she just met, while a man she just fucked stands across the room.

Oh sweet Jesus.

My sister is something else. Her ability to jump from man to man astonishes me, but it shouldn't. I've watched her do it since the day she realized her tits had superpowers.

"I'm Luna," she says, extending a hand to the

man who had his face so close to my vagina he could legally be my husband in many countries. "Rosie's twin."

"It's a pleasure to meet you," he says, taking her hand in his.

Luna's entire being moves toward him like she's drawn to the handsome doctor by an invisible force.

"You too, Doc." She smiles, lifting one shoulder, being super flirty.

They stare at each other, the air crackling with electricity and hope. I've witnessed the behavior more times than I can count from men, but I've never seen my sister reciprocate it until now.

Oh boy.

I lean over, putting my mouth near her ear as she finally lowers her ass back to my bed. "Do not fuck my doctor," I whisper so only she can hear.

"I can't make any promises," she says back but not quietly and with her eyes still on the tall, dark, and handsome man standing in scrubs. "He's too delish."

Dr. Sinclair smirks, staring right at her and not put off by her forwardness one bit. This is going to be trouble. My sister will no doubt wreck this man, and I'll be in search of a new doctor before I've barely settled in at home with Sal.

"I just wanted to check on you and the baby before I headed out for the evening."

"I'm sure your wife is waiting for you," Luna says,

casting her reel and fishing for a man right after banging the last.

"No," he says, the smile on his face widening because players always recognize the game. "No wife."

"Shame," she says with a small pout.

I roll my eyes.

"We're great, Doc," I interject, ready for the two of them to stop the virtual eye-banging they're doing to each other. "All good to go."

He dips his chin at me, snapping my chart closed. "Great to hear. If you need anything, don't hesitate to call," he says, but those words are spoken while his eyes are pinned on Luna and not me.

"Fucking hell," I mutter under my breath before I clear my throat, trying to break up their fixation. "Thank you, Dr. Sinclair."

"I may be in need of your services," she says to him.

"Your sister has my cell. Feel free to call me if you need anything."

"I will," she says, winking at him.

I close my eyes, both praying for patience and out of sheer mortification.

"Good night," he says to us.

As soon as he's gone, I turn to her and shake my head.

"What?" she asks, jerking her head back.

"You seriously just fucked Ian, and now you're trying to get in the pants of my doctor," I whisper and tick my head toward Dylan and his brother. "How do you think he feels right now?"

Ian laughs. "Pretty fucking good, actually. What your sister and I had was beautiful and special…"

I snort at the ridiculousness of the two of them.

"But we made no promises of love to each other. We were just passing time and having some fun," Ian continues, but I don't believe a word he's saying. I see the way he looks at my sister, and if any man is in love, it's him.

"I pass time by reading a book," I tell them, but I shouldn't be surprised by their behavior or their words.

"You really missed out on a lot of fun, Ro."

"Nope. I'm happy she'd rather bury her face in a book than…" Dylan winces, no doubt recoiling at the thought of me with another man. "She missed out on nothing."

"Your loss." Luna shrugs and then nudges me with her shoulder. "Now, I'm going to need that phone number."

"You're such a…"

Luna raises her eyebrows. "I'm sure that man knows a woman's body like the back of his hand. A girl has to explore and experience everything."

"Thank God I have a son," Dylan says, walking back toward the bed and sitting on the opposite side from Luna. "I don't think I'd survive a daughter."

I lean over, resting my head on his shoulder as I stare down at our baby boy. "You better brace yourself, honey. I want a girl someday."

"Fuck," he hisses. "You want to torture me, don't you?"

"There's nothing like the love a little girl has for her father."

He kisses the top of my head and murmurs, "I'll miss you."

I peer up at him. "Where you going?"

"I have no doubt I'll land in prison before she's eighteen. Too many assholes in the world."

I chuckle, relaxing back into him. "Not all men are bad."

"Yeah. We are, and I don't think anyone will be good enough for my children."

"You'll let go eventually," I tell him, yawning longer this time as my eyes grow heavy.

"I'm never letting go of my family," he says as I close my eyes, allowing the sleep and happiness to take me under. Life doesn't get any better than this.

Thank you for reading Ashes. Are you ready for more Men of Inked Heatwave? Luna Gallo never does anything the easy way and that includes love. Don't miss her crazy sexy tale in Scorch. Learn more at menofinked.com/scorch

LETTER FROM CHELLE

Dear Gallo Girl or Guy,

Thank you for reading Ashes, Rosie Gallo's story. I hope you love Dylan and Rosie as much as I do and I hope you're ready for more Gallo goodness because there's so much left to be told.

It's been an interesting few months and I'm utterly and completely exhausted. We moved back to our hometown in Ohio after living in Florida for the last fifteen years. With this move I realized I'm no longer a young person, but older, slower, and weaker than at any other point in my adult life.

I'm tired. So so tired, but I'm happy to be back home, surrounded by my family and maybe able to take another nap soon.

We had our first snow fall last week and it was beautiful. The wonder of the puffy flakes floating to the ground will wear off on me super quick. Watching it from the comfort of my home is one thing, but going out in it…is another.

So goodbye sunshine. Hello gray skies.

I'm busy setting up my new office because I'm ready to write. I need to write. The Gallos are calling to me and they're not a group that can be ignored.

By the time this book releases Christmas will be over and we'll be a few days into 2022. I hope this year will bring you peace, happiness, and prosperity. After the last two years, we deserve a damn break.

Take care of yourself my old friend. Be kind to yourself and make time for you.

Much love —

Chelle Bliss xoxoxo

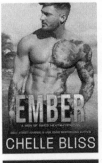

ABOUT THE AUTHOR

I'm a full-time writer, time-waster extraordinaire, social media addict, coffee fiend, and ex-history teacher. *To learn more about my books, please visit menofinked.com.*

Want to stay up-to-date on the newest Men of Inked release and more? Join my newsletter.

Join over 10,000 readers on Facebook in Chelle Bliss Books private reader group and talk books and all things reading. Come be part of the family!

See the Gallo Family Tree

Where to Follow Me:

facebook.com/authorchellebliss1

instagram.com/authorchellebliss

bookbub.com/authors/chelle-bliss

goodreads.com/chellebliss

amazon.com/author/chellebliss

twitter.com/ChelleBliss1

pinterest.com/chellebliss10

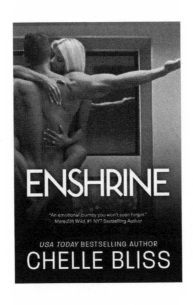

"**Beautiful**. **Poignant**. This book will stay with you long after you've finished." ~ RACHEL VAN DYKEN, #1 NYT BESTSELLING AUTHOR

"An **emotional journey** you won't soon forget." ~ MEREDITH WILD, #1 NYT BESTSELLING AUTHOR

Tap here to learn more about Enshrine or visit menofinked.com/enshrine for more info.

MEN OF INKED SERIES

"One of the sexiest series of all-time" -Bookbub Reviewers
Download book 1 for FREE!

- Book 1 - Throttle Me (Joe aka City)
- Book 2 - Hook Me (Mike)
- Book 3 - Resist Me (Izzy)
- Book 4 - Uncover Me (Thomas)
- Book 5 - Without Me (Anthony)
- Book 6 - Honor Me (City)
- Book 7 - Worship Me (Izzy)

MEN OF INKED: SOUTHSIDE SERIES

Join the Chicago Gallo Family with their strong alphas,
sassy women, and tons of fun.

- Book 1 - Maneuver (Lucio)
- Book 2 - Flow (Daphne)
- Book 3 - Hook (Angelo)
- Book 4 - Hustle (Vinnie)
- Book 5 - Love (Angelo)

MEN OF INKED: HEATWAVE SERIES

Same Family. New Generation.

- Book 1 - Flame (Gigi)
- Book 2 - Burn (Gigi)
- Book 3 - Wildfire (Tamara)
- Book 4 - Blaze (Lily)
- Book 5 - Ignite (Tamara)
- Book 6 - Spark (Nick)
- Book 7 - Ember (Rocco)
- Book 8 - Singe - (Carmello)
- Book 9 - Ashes - (Rosie)
- Book 10 - Scorch - (Luna)

ALFA INVESTIGATIONS SERIES

Wickedly hot alphas with tons of heart pounding suspense!

- Book 1 - Sinful Intent (Morgan)
- Book 2 - Unlawful Desire (Frisco)
- Book 3 - Wicked Impulse (Bear)
- Book 4 - Guilty Sin (Ret)

SINGLE READS

- Mend
- Enshrine
- Misadventures of a City Girl
- Misadventures with a Speed Demon

- Rebound (Flash aka Sam)
- Top Bottom Switch (Ret)
- Santa Baby
- Fearless - (Austin Moore)

View Chelle's entire collection of books at menofinked.com/books

To learn more about Chelle's books visit *menofinked.com* or *chellebliss.com*

Made in the USA
Middletown, DE
14 May 2022